TROUBLE THE WATER

NICOLE SEITZ

THOMAS NELSON

Since 1798

NASHVILLE   DALLAS   MEXICO CITY   RIO DE JANEIRO   BEIJING

Published in Nashville, Tennessee, by Thomas Nelson. Thomas Nelson is a registered trademark of Thomas Nelson, Inc.

Thomas Nelson books may be purchased in bulk for educational, business, fund-raising, or sales promotional use. For information, please e-mail SpecialMarkets@ThomasNelson.com.

Grateful acknowledgement is made for the following resources that provided information on Gullah/Geechee culture and on care for the dying:

Ring shout lyrics adapted from "Run Old Jeremiah." Source: *Afro-American Spirituals, Work Songs, and Ballads*, ed. Alan Lomax (Washington, D.C.: Library of Congress Archive of Folk Song, AFS L3). Sung by Joe Washington Brown and Austin Coleman at Jennings, Louisiana, 1934. Recorded by John A. and Alan Lomax.

"Saying Goodbye" excerpts adapted from Brochure 3 of the Complete Life series, *Care for the Dying: Preparing to Say Goodbye*, Center on Aging, John A. Burns School of Medicine, University of Hawaii, 2002.

Scripture quotation marked KJV is taken from The King James Version of the Bible.

Publisher's Note: This novel is a work of fiction. Names, characters, places, and incidents are either products of the author's imagination or used fictitiously. All characters are fictional, and any similarity to people living or dead is purely coincidental.

Page Design by Casey Hooper

Library of Congress Cataloging in Publication Data
Seitz, Nicole A.
  Trouble the water / Nicole Seitz.
    p. cm.
  ISBN 978-1-59554-400-1 (softcover)
  1. Middle-aged women--Fiction. 2. Domestic fiction. I. Title.
PS3619.E426T76 2008
813'.6--dc22

2007051520

Printed in the United States of America
08 09 10 11 RRD 6 5 4 3

Acknowledgments

I am grateful first to God for giving me the wisdom to recognize that some endings are actually new beginnings. To my aunt, Bonnie Marie Furr Buck, this book could not have been written without you. You left your colorful marks in this world, in my life, and I thank you for pulling your heavenly strings. I look forward to seeing you again one day.

I thank my mother, Miriam Furr Lucas, for being my greatest support and inspiration. Words just can't do you justice. And to my stepfather, Hollis Lucas Jr., I thank you for believing in me. Your love has made every difference in my life. To my husband,

Brian, you're the kindest, most amazing man I've ever met. How could I ever do this without you? And to my children, Olivia and Cole, you make me want to be a better person. There is no greater gift than this.

I am blessed to be with the folks at Thomas Nelson who understand the power of the written word. To Allen Arnold and Amanda Bostic, thank you for believing in me and supporting me as an author. To Mark Ross, Carrie Wagner, Ami McConnell, Natalie Hanemann, Jennifer Deshler, Sandy Bradley, and Lisa Young, I'm so glad I've landed in your talented hands. Your passion is infectious. To my agent, Mark Gilroy, thanks to you I actually have people who read my little stories. God bless you. And to Rachelle Gardner, you are an amazing editor—you truly "get me" as a writer, and you make my words shine. Thank you, thank you.

I've been honored to work again with Queen Quet, Chieftess of the Gullah/Geechee Nation, in my efforts to portray the Gullah language and customs as accurately as possible. Queen Quet, thank you so much for your support. You are truly one in a million. Also, my sincere thanks goes to Pat Conroy for planting the seed for this novel in my head. Your brilliance is only outweighed by your kindness.

Since the release of my first novel, *The Spirit of Sweetgrass,* many have gone to bat for me, working hard to get the word out about this new writer: my parents, my aunt, Barbara Furr, my parents-in-law, Dave and Judy Seitz, Jill Coley of the *Post* and *Courier,* and Ric Cochran of Charleston, WV's V100-FM. Many South Carolina bookstores have championed my work as well: Barnes and Noble in Mount Pleasant and Charleston, Waldenbooks in Charleston and Columbia, Litchfield Books in Pawley's Island, and Books-A-Millions all over the Southeast. I'm indebted to you all!

To Fred Robinson, Irene Lofton, George Pope and everyone in the Seacoast Christian Writers' Group, your friendship and support sustain me. I could never ask for a more talented group of cheerleaders. And to Red Evans, congratulations on your first book, *On Ice*! Thanks for bringing Eldridge Brewer into this world. We're better for it.

To you, my dear reader whose life or family has been affected in some way by cancer—my prayers go out to you. Look up and know there are mansions in the sky. Last but not least, family means everything. To my sister, Andrea Bell, and my brother, David Bensch—both whom I love with all my heart—and to sisters and siblings everywhere, well, this one's for you.

For Bonnie and Sister

For an angel went down at a certain season into the pool, and troubled the water: whosoever then first after the troubling of the water stepped in was made whole of whatsoever disease he had.

—JOHN 5:4 KJV

Prologue

St. Anne's Isle, South Carolina

June 4, 2008

Duchess

When the mood strikes me, the moon is just right, and the ocean behind my home is calm and calling me, I obey it and come. Just like Mama taught me to, quick and with no lip—I come, body naked, soul bared, water flowing 'round my waist—and once again I am seventeen, innocent, unashamed. Not stuck in this sixty-some-odd-year-old body that plumps and hangs whichever way it pleases. No. In those sweet moments I am Youth again. She's still there inside me, that beautiful girl. So why not let the little booger out every now and again?

Have you ever been skinny-dipping? My first time was as a teenager, gorgeous and oblivious to what the world had in store for me. These days, I suppose a woman my age really should *not* bare all—that's what folks would have you think, anyway. But you know what I say to those folks? Kiss my nice white behind, slightly tanned. Yes ma'am.

I've come to accept my body. And that's saying a lot. My tummy makes it hard for me to paint my toenails, and my rear has stretched to somewhere 'round mid-thigh. But the thing that really gets me is the looseness under my neck. I feel that soft waddle and wonder who the heck has taken over, like one of those alien movies where they grow up out of bean pods.

No, sadly, it's me. I'm showing my years. I could say I've lived life for all it's worth, but to tell the truth, about half the time it's plumb lived me to death. I'm still here though to tell about it, which is mighty amazing if you ask me. Because I haven't always wanted to be here, in this life, that is. But a very special young lady—one that reminded me so much of myself—came to visit a couple years ago, and Lord bless her heart, she changed all that.

I can still remember the look on her face when we met! Her green eyes bugged and darted away fast like a child staring at the sun, sweet thing. I wanted to giggle so bad, but I kept control of myself—I've had years of learning to stuff down true emotion. That, and the fact I'd seen this look of shock before. See, I'd just come back from skinny-dipping and was still naked as a jaybird when the door swung open. There she was—my angel—she'd finally arrived.

Honor painted me a whole new view on life, and I hope I did the same for her. We were kindred spirits, Honor and me. She touched me and all at once knew me. And as the day is long, I know I'll never meet another Honor Maddox. The child was like a daughter to me.

Now I may not know a lot, and people may poke fun at me— I know they do, snickering, making jokes, calling me names— but that's all right. Because when Honor met me I was a mess, my goodness. And today, well, I'm not perfect, far from it, but better off. And you know I'm not a 'specially religious person, but I'm pretty sure The Man Above had something to do with Honor finding me. See, He's crafty like that. I don't put anything past Him.

I'm not only older, I'm wiser now too—and this is what I know for a fact: there are angels who can enter your life every now and again whether man, woman, or puppy dog, and leave their sweet little paw prints all over your life. If you want my humble advice, tell 'em, "Come in! Come in!" like I did with Honor that fine summer day—into my home and deepest darkest nooks and crannies. The opening-up part can be scary as the dickens, but when you meet a true angel, let me tell you, you're never the same. Problem is, you can only see angels in brief glimpses like stars poking out from behind the clouds. The days I shared with Honor were numbered and just too few.

This is another thing I know for a fact: a woman can't be an island, not really. No, it's the touching we do in other people's lives that matters when all is said and done. The silly things we do for ourselves—shiny new cars and jobs and money—they don't mean a hill of beans. Honor taught me that. My soul sisters on this island taught me that. And this is the story of true sisterhood. It's the story of Honor, come and gone, and how one flawed woman worked miracles in this mixed-up world.

There's something truly magical about St. Anne's Isle. It's a place full of sand and saltwater, marsh grass and colorful people—all the things that give a place its soul. St. Anne's surely has one. A soul, that is. Or rather, many of 'em. Souls are drawn here from all over the place. I was—came as a little girl, spending my summer times here with Mama and Daddy. We lived inland the rest of the year where mosquitoes bit like the dickens and ocean breezes never blew.

I came back to St. Anne's when I was able and made it my home. I missed how the sand felt, blowing over my naked feet. I missed the Gullahs who seemed to know me better than I did myself. And then Honor came—she was drawn here too. The island pulled her like a lighthouse, guiding her through rocky seas.

Honor came to me in the most unusual way. Our meeting was coincidental, or maybe it wasn't—I'm tending to think now it was all meant to happen, every speck. 'Course, that's the magic of this place, like I was saying.

It pains me to say these words, but Lord knows I got to get it out. I'm gonna take great care to tell it just like it happened—to me, to Honor, God rest her sweet soul. So listen up close now. I doubt after all this is said and done I can ever rehash it again.

1

St. Anne's Isle, Two years earlier
July 13, 2006

Honor

It was late in the afternoon, and I was sitting very still, listening to the crickets and frogs begin their chanting—they were telling me the time had come. The humid air was settling in around me, pressing me into the wood slats of the bench like straps to a gurney. It was going to be the perfect night for what I needed to do.

I'd been going there to the playground to paint for months. I knew which children were spoiled. I knew which ones missed their mothers during the day. And I knew their black nannies were raising them while their white mamas and daddies were off making more money. And I'd come there thinking that was the kind of life I wanted. On this day, I realized I was fooling myself again—being one of them was no better than being me. But one thing was certain. I couldn't stand being me any longer.

The playground was finally empty.

I'd set my painting down on the bench and folded my easel, laying it on the ground. The sun had ducked behind the trees, and it was turning dark quickly. I'd always loved that time of day—just before the dark comes and engulfs us all in an equalizing, masking blackness where no one can see just how beautiful or ugly we are.

"Where is it?" A shrill voice broke my silence. "Do you see it? I can't see it!"

A little girl in pigtails dragged her nanny by the wrist. *What is she, a slave?* I thought. *Give her a break already.*

"We have to find it!"

"Chile, you are gettin' too old for that thing. You ain't a baby no more."

"Waaahhh!"

"Hush! Hush now. Lookee-here. I got it. Baby, hush. It's right here, now come on. Your mama's gonna be home soon."

I watched the pair traipse out of the sand box with a filthy blanket in tow. I wondered, why in the world did she hold on to that thing? *Get a grip, honey. Life's hard. You can't take that blanket with you forever, you know.* Of course I thought that—just as I was twisting my old wedding band on my finger. *Well, what the heck. Maybe you can always have your pacifier blankie, sugar. Go right ahead. Be my guest.* I took the ring off and dropped it over my shoulder. It landed with a tiny thud on the ground.

I suppose it must have been the skip in that little girl's stride or maybe her blonde hair dancing in the fading light, but all of a sudden I thought of you.

Alice!

Oh no. Alice. And the girls! What's this going to do to them? Will they suffer? Will they miss me?

No. They're going to be fine, I reasoned. *They barely know I exist anymore. I'm out of sight, out of mind.* I must have wanted it that way though, hadn't I? Deep down, I think that's really what I must have wanted—to leave you and the girls before you didn't love me anymore. Before you found out who I really was.

The color crimson caught my eye, and I glanced at my painting. It was a self-portrait. Surprise. Whoopee. They all were recently, and they were all atrocious. I'd tried different colors, different angles, oils, pastels, acrylics—me on the beach, me on a cloud, me on a park bench—I'd only get the same result. *But this is the last one,* I told myself. I titled it "Anonymous." *I do not know this person on the canvas. I do not know the person behind my eyes. Even God won't look at me anymore.*

I bent my head back and stared at the hazy sky, searching for rising stars. *Oh God, I have failed. You know how badly I've failed. I am so sorry, for the last time. I cannot do anything more. I am just so tired.* My eyelids pressed shut and tears began streaming. "Don't do this," I pleaded out loud. "Don't you dare cry! You don't deserve to cry. There will be no tears at your funeral, Honor Maddox. No tears! None at all!"

In my final moments, I breathed in deeply. I exhaled one last "goodbye" to no one in particular, to everyone, to you and your sweet girls, to the world. I closed my eyes. *I'm getting sleepy. I'm very sleepy. I'm going. I'm coming, God. I'm so sleepy. I can't feel my toes, my fingers, my nose. I'm in oblivion. Ashes to ashes and dust to dust. Our Father who art in heaven, hallowed be—*

"You goin' to sleep here?"

Huh? Wha—

"Missy, you're fallin' asleep. You best wake up now and go on home. You all right? You feelin' all right? It's gettin' dark."

Are you kidding me?

I cracked my eyelids and stared up. In the dim light of the moon, I saw a large round mass above me. It was one of the nannies I'd seen so many times before but had never spoken to. Her head was wrapped in a green printed cloth and tied at the front, above her brow. Her arms were thick, nearly leg-sized, and her hands, large, like a man's. She was nudging me hard in the ribs.

"Lady? Miss? You all right? You sick? You ain't sick are you? Go on and sit up now."

She pulled on my arms, and I struggled to rise. *Ugh. I thought everyone was gone. I'm so tired . . . enough already.*

As luck would have it, when I moved to sitting, my hand hit the empty medicine bottle, causing it to roll onto the ground and smack into her foot. The woman bent down, picked it up and squinted at it, lifting her eyeglasses to try and read in the moonlight. "You ain't took them pills, did you?"

"Maybe a couple," I slurred.

"Oh Lord in heaven! Oh God Almighty! Aaaaaagh! Aaaaaagh! Lord in heaven!" The woman danced around on tiptoes like a hippo in the Nutcracker, pulling at her hair and unraveling her head wrap. Her black hair underneath was matted on one side and wild and fuzzy on the other. "Got to get help! *Help! Help! Heeeeelp!*" She ran back and forth with hands waving as if trying to conjure someone out of thin air.

God, I did not want all this drama. Truly. Can I just go in peace? Is that too much to ask?

I lay back down on the bench and watched the woman's dance as my eyes began to close again. *This feels so good. Yes. This is right. It'll all be over soon. No more pity in their eyes. They always have pity when they look at me. They say I'm beautiful and wonderful, but they're all liars. I'm just so tired.*

Is she gone? Hallelujah. Now I lay me down to sleep, I pray the Lord my soul to keep. If I should die before I wake, I pray the Lord my soul to take. Bless Mama and Daddy, and Alice and . . .

"There she is! There she is! Whooooo! She still there! Is she dead? Oh Lordy Jesus, don't let that lady die! Don't let her die, don't let her *die!*"

My arms tingled. I heard voices. *Angels? Are they coming for me?*

"Oh sweet baby, don't you worry. You gonna be all right. My

name's Ruby. Miss Blondell's gonna take good care o' you. Just hold on. Don't you die now." Seemed a munchkin had me now. She picked up my left foot and then the other, sliding them off the bench. "Willa, grab her right here," she said, pointing at my face. "Good. I got her down here. No, *no!* Hold her haid up."

"I got it!"

"You got it?"

"I got it, Ruby. Go on, now. Git! *Oh, Lord Jesus in heaven, have mercy on this chile. Sweet Father in heaven, don't let this chile die in my arms.* Nooooo sir. You just keep on a-living 'cause ain't no white girl gonna die in Willa's arms. No sir. You just breathe in and let go that hand o' the dead. The livin' pullin' you back here, chile. You just hold on now, 'cause we gonna pull you on back."

Oh, you've got to be kidding me. My limbs felt like I was being ripped apart as they joggled my body. *Just kill me already. Please, I'm so tired.*

I'm not sure how long they carried me—I lost count of how many times my feet were dropped on the ground and dragged. After a while I couldn't hear the sounds of nature anymore, the crickets and whippoorwills, or feel the dampness of night. Finally there was a hard thump on my back. *Maybe they've finished me off? They did. Thank God. The crazy black women finally had pity and whacked the life right out of me.*

Ow! *Have mercy!* They did it again.

"Not so hard, Ruby. Not so hard. You wanna kill the girl already?"

"But shouldn't it be workin' by now? How much you give her, Blondell?"

"I gib her 'nough. Sit tigh."

"Ah Lawd have mercy, I *knew* this ain't good. Gawd in heaven, why we ain't took her to a hospital? Lawd, Christ!"

"Watch yo' mouth, Ruby."

Quiet. Then wailing. Then pacing. My mind was numb, my body swollen with cotton, but I could tell I was indoors by the cold, hard floor and bright light. I could hear water running in another room while my head rested on the cool edge of a toilet seat. Then I felt a sudden churning in my stomach and the vilest pain I'd ever encountered. "Aaaaaaaagh! Gaaarrrgh!"

"There, there, now. Just let it all out. Let all that poison out. Ruby's right here, so you just let it all out now. That's it. Pank! Them pills was pank, Blondell. Aw no. Aw no. That ain't blood, is it? Aaaaaw Lawd have mercy, have mercy, sweet Jesus!"

The little one who'd been stroking my hair peeled away and fainted dead on the floor next to me. My stomach belched one final blast of liquid and bile and then . . . I waited . . . I waited . . . nothing. I rested my head on my arm, sweating. I stunk. The toilet stunk. I heard it flush and watched as my latest attempt to kill myself swirled down the drain along with every ounce of desire for living and any sense of accomplishment for actually going through with it this time.

I don't *want to live. Why is that so hard? God, I would* like *to come up to heaven now, so I would appreciate it if You'd just get me*

out of this crazy black lady's house and hit me hard and fast with
a speeding vehicle as I leave. Okay? Can You do that please? Is that
too much to ask?

I was too tired to cry. I would have if I could have, but I was
just too tired. There was vomit in my nostrils. My stomach muscles were sore. With everything I had in me, I rolled over and
propped myself up in the corner next to the toilet. The white
tiles beneath me were cracked and the grout mildewed. The
wallpaper must have been from 1947. It was faded and peeling
back in long flimsy strips.

There was a black woman in front of me, wiping my face
with a wet washcloth. *Oh, that feels good. Mother used to do that.*
I opened my eyes again. It wasn't Mama. It was the woman with
lopsided hair and man-sized features. Her dark eyes were puffy
from crying behind her glasses.

"You all right now, baby. Willa here now. God knew to turn
me back to the park tonight. Ain't sure what I was goin' for, but
I know it now. I come for you, chile." Her hand brushed my
cheek. "Yessir. He brung you to the right place is what He done.
You need healin', chile. By the grace of God, He brung you to the
right place. Miss Blondell always know what she doin'. Ruby, get
on off the flo' and grab me a glass o' water, hear?"

Cold water touched my lips, and I let it run down my chin.
She wiped it up off my neck. An ancient, wiry woman came
from the kitchen and bent to her knees, leaning in close. The
smell of onions and fresh greens seeped from her skin.

"Such a shame. Sure is a pretty thing," said the one cradling my head and clucking her tongue.

"Migh' look nice outside, Willa, but ain on de inside. Ain dat righ', baby? What you do wrong, chile? Ain nuttin you can do dat Gawd ain gwine forgive. No sir. You gwine be awright. Go on now, fetch some fresh sheet and pilla out de closet. Hurry now. Ruby, come on in ya and help move een de bedroom."

They lifted me to standing, but my legs were too heavy. Can a dead woman walk? The floorboards creaked. I put all my weight on the three women carrying me and then fell onto the bed like a baby bird out of the nest. *I tried to fly. Really I did. I'm just not cut out for it.*

Oh, thank God. This is my final resting place, I thought—*cool white clouds of heaven nestled under me and over me. This is all I've ever wanted. Peace and quiet. Now I lay me down to sleep.* The light flicked out and there was total darkness. It rolled all around me and painted me black.

I'm dead. Finally. Thank God.

2

Honor

"Inky, git down ya," a voice came at me from a few feet away. "Cat always up in folk bizness. Shoo, cat. Gw'on." I felt a wet scratchy kiss on my cheek. It took a few licks to open my eyes, and then there it was in the hazy morning light—the biggest black cat I'd ever seen. His eyes were bright yellow and kind. I stared into them thinking stupidly, *Gee, I never expected to see cats in heaven.*

The cat jumped away when a tall figure with drooping shoulders and a stern face walked toward me. I remembered that face from the night before, hovering over me, making me drink something awful. Seeing her, I knew I was alive, and a shot of panic flew through me. Memories of the playground, the pills, the nannies, started flooding back.

"What yo name, chile?" The woman's face was worn leather, her skin the color of burnt sugar. Her lips were round and large with the bottom one hanging low, leaving a small gaping hole even when her mouth was shut.

"Honor," I croaked, finding my voice.

Her lips tightened as she assessed me, then she leaned over and used her finger to wipe something on my forehead.

"Honor, where from?" she asked.

"H . . . here. Well, originally Murrells Inlet."

The woman stared at me blankly as if she didn't quite understand.

"You know, the seafood capital of South Carolina?" I attempted levity and even a smile, but she closed her eyes then and rolled her head back, mumbling something under her breath, chanting it seemed. Praying.

The room around me was small and dingy blue. I was lying in a tall queen bed that nearly took up the entire room except for a pinewood dresser covered in knickknacks and Bibles, some opened and flagged, others closed and stacked.

The woman cracked her eyelids and stared at me, unconcerned. "Git up now. Time ta eat." She walked to the window and pushed back white sheers. Then she lifted the window with everything in her. I watched as her arm muscles strained and she inhaled the cool breeze streaming in. I couldn't decide if she was sixty or a hundred, for she appeared extremely fragile yet strong as an ox.

I didn't say a word, but instead obeyed the woman. Had I really tried to kill myself? Worse, had I actually been caught trying?

I sat on the edge of the bed and looked down at my legs. I was wearing the same outfit I'd chosen the day before—it was to be my death attire—my finest black slacks that had a nice slimming effect and a gold sequined top I'd only worn once to a New Year's Eve party. I grimaced at my dirty bare feet.

I was a beached whale. It took great effort to roll my limbs onto the floor, and when I did, I swear I'd gained a hundred pounds. My head was a swarm of bees. My eyes covered in putty.

"Ain got aw day," the woman fussed. "Wash up now, ya?" Then her voice lowered as she walked through the door, and I couldn't understand anymore. Touching the walls, I felt my way down a very narrow hallway over a long, faded rug that was curled up on the edges. My arm reached through a doorway for the light switch. I flicked it on and then squinted at the very place where my life had been saved the night before. Everything was illuminated in a bright yellow omniscience. I stared down at the toilet I'd clung to so dearly. It was a tiny porcelain bowl so low to the ground that I had to hold on to the basin sink beside me just to lower myself and keep from falling in.

I sat there for a while but couldn't go. I was dehydrated, my mouth pasty and thick with an acrid taste. I finally stood at the sink in front of a round tarnished mirror. "You really did it this time, Honor," my reflection said. "I gotta hand it to you. Another doozy."

I stuck out my white tongue. My eyes were bloodshot and wrinkled, and my highlighted hair was somehow unable to hide my gray any longer. There were garish makeup smudges down my cheeks. Shucks, I'd made myself up so deliberately the day before. It had been my finest work as if painting my masterpiece. And yet here I was—a canvas left out in the rain.

"Ain got aw day, chile!" I heard pots clanking.

"Coming," I answered, rushing now. I washed my face and gargled with a dab of toothpaste and water, and followed the smell of strong coffee into the living room. There was a little brown sofa with a tattered blanket and pillow strewn on it. Had the old woman slept here overnight? I turned around and faced the bedroom. There was only one bedroom! I'd taken the woman's bed! I thought I might die right then and there.

I watched her standing at the kitchen sink. She kept her back toward me while cutting vegetables slowly and deliberately as if she feared she may cut herself or perhaps had arthritis. I stared at those knives with the longing of an alcoholic for whiskey. They were large and sharp and could end my life so quickly.

"Sit," she said, seeing me watching her. So I sat.

Her kitchen table was one of those old-fashioned diner kinds with the white vinyl top and metal bands around the sides. The chairs were the same. As I lowered onto one, it made an embarrassing gassy noise as the air squeezed out. I flushed and then became gratefully distracted by what I saw across from me.

The big black cat who had licked me awake was sitting in the opposite chair, his hindquarters on the seat and his paws on the table. The cat's nose was buried in a saucer of milk. "Well, hello again," I said, embarrassed by the sound of my own voice. He looked up at me nonchalantly and moved his tongue from side to side, grabbing droplets of milk from his whiskers. He lifted his paw and licked it, then wiped his face repeatedly in a cleansing ritual. Apparently satisfied he'd done all he needed, the cat lumbered off the chair and found a place near the window on the hardwood floor where the sunlight had formed a square blanket.

My stomach was churning, and I held it gingerly. The woman crept over, carrying a cup and saucer that rattled as she walked. She sat the cup in front of me, turning the chipped side away, and then she poured steaming black coffee from her pot, filling it all the way to the top.

She must have seen me eyeing the cup and looking around for cream because she said, "Ain no milk. Don't need it." Well now, she and I both knew I'd just witnessed the cat drinking some, and I glanced at his saucer still half full on the table.

"Cat need milk. Woman need strong black coffee! Coffee like life. Ain no waterin' it down."

I picked up the cup to hide my lips and inhale its richness. Black coffee. No fluff, no sugar. Now there was a concept. I closed my eyes and puckered my mouth. It burned the dickens

out of my lips when they touched the edge, but it *was* good coffee. The best cup I'd ever had. In that instant, with warmth
rolling down to my insides, a thought, a flash hit me: *I'm glad
I'm not dead so that I can enjoy this.* Isn't that simple? It was such
a simple thought that I assumed it meant nothing.

The cat stirred first before anyone knocked. I watched his
head lift and ears go straight, and then heard a light tapping on
the door. The old lady didn't notice, or if she did, she didn't make
it known. She kept cutting vegetables rhythmically, the cadence
sending me into a slight trance. "Would you like me to . . . I'll just
go get that." Detecting a slight nod from her, I got up to answer
the door.

There were two women on the other side. One was a large,
round woman about my height with a kind face, glasses, and
carefully curled hair. She was dark-skinned and I guessed about
my age, forty-five. I recognized her thick wrists from the night
before. They'd carried my weight. Now they were carrying a
sweetgrass basket filled with breads and jams.

"Well good mornin', sunshine! So nice to see you up already.
You give us quite a scare, you know. Had me up prayin' for you
all night long. Ain't no matter. You lookin' fine today. My name's
Willa, if you cain't remember," she said moving past me and
straight for the kitchen.

"I'm Ruby," squeaked a little woman standing in the doorway.
She was the size of a peanut with a voice to match, wearing tight
blue jeans and big loop earrings. Her hair was cropped short, and

it was truly hard to know if she was a child or an adult. "I just dropped Tyrone off to school, Blondell," she yelled in the door, "so you got me all day if you need me." Well, there was my answer. She was a mother—or a nanny—but certainly not a child. It would take some getting used to, being around someone so petite.

"Hey Ruby. Please tek Missy oba ta Duchess house, ya."

"Duchess? Really?" Blondell didn't respond, just stared at her. "Okay then. Lawd have mercy," she said, turning to me. "Wait till you meet Duchess. That woman so crazy even the firemens know not to come when she call. I reckon Miss Blondell gonna sic her on you though. She don't take too kindly to folks killin' theyselves."

"I'm sorry I . . . caused so much trouble last night. It's silly, really, today. I . . . I'll just be going, and thank you so much again, for your kindness. All of you."

I spotted my shoes by the doorway and made a beeline for them.

The house grew completely silent—uncomfortably so—as if it weren't that way already.

"I'll just go make the bed now." I slipped on my shoes and slid back to the bedroom. I pulled the sheets up around the pillow and then thought better of it. *I really should wash these sheets for her. She gave me her only bed. She gave me coffee. She saved my life, for goodness sake.* I stripped them off and bundled them up under my arm and then entered the living room slowly. The women were huddled around the kitchen sink, whispering.

The large one, Willa, turned to face me.

"I'm just going to take these and wash them," I told her. It was only then that I remembered I had no place to wash. And no money to my name. *Dad-gum! I knew I was killing myself for a reason! People just don't do that when things are good.* I had no job, no money, and I'd just been kicked out of my meager housing. It all rushed back to me, and my face must have gone beet red because Willa stepped forward and took my hand.

"I don't mean to be unkind," she said, "but it seems to me, you in a bad way. Maybe you need to talk to somebody 'bout what's hurtin' up inside. You can talk to me if you want to."

"Oh no! I'm fine," I said, pulling my fingers from her grasp. "Really, I'm fine. I just needed to clear my head. I'm not sure what got into me. I've never, ever done anything so silly in all my life. It's just so unlike me. I'll just be going now."

I was beginning to giggle out of nervousness when Blondell turned around and said, "Sit." So again, I sat.

She clucked her tongue and the black cat perked his ears. He stood up, stretched, and then curled himself around her leg. Blondell tapped the chair and he jumped up in it, then she grabbed him in her arms and stroked him. "Seem like you need some tings—a place ta stay, food ta eat. You gwine yonda ta Duchess' house." She cocked her head toward the window. "You gwine meet we nannies een de park eb'ry day, noon. We nannies, we gwine talk to you den."

I wasn't quite sure what the woman had said, but I was in red alarm. I must have appeared confused because Willa began to interpret for me.

"Miss Blondell wants you to stay over at Duchess' house for a while," she explained. "And she wants you to come to the play park every day at noon, well, like you was doin'. 'Cept this time, you gonna be in our circle."

"Circle?" I repeated.

"The nannies," chimed Ruby in her tiny voice. "We meet every day in the same place. We all get together and have a good ol' time, talking 'bout our day, talking 'bout our chill'ren. Miss Blondell say she gonna come now too. That's a big thang 'cause she don't come 'round much no more. She's takin' you on, Miss . . . what's your name?"

"Honor."

"Miss Honor. Miss Blondell wants to take you on, and I'd listen to her if I was you. She know what she doin'. She pretty much raised me."

"And me too," said Willa.

"Take me on?" *Like a project? Like a child?* "No offense. I am grateful for last night, but I am no one's project. I'm sorry, I've really got to go. If y'all will please excuse me."

"Y'ain't got no place to go, do you, Miss Honor?" asked Ruby.

"Well, I, of course. I have family."

"So you goin' to see your family now? They in town?" Ruby was becoming a pest.

"They're not here, they're—" I thought of you, Alice, but I

couldn't imagine going to see you in Murrells Inlet. Not this way. Not in this state of mind. I would become the greatest drain on you, a burden, your psychopathic sister. "I just need to go," I said. "Thank you. Very much. I wish you all the best."

I had the door swung open with one foot on the porch when I heard a rusty voice say one phrase that made my skin crawl.

"Ruby, call de po-lease."

I turned slowly and faced Blondell. Willa and Ruby were cowering behind her, and that big black cat was curling his tail around her arm.

"You leave now, gwine call de po-lease. What you da do ain right a'tall! Ain nobody pose ta kill eself. You owe me. Best do as I say."

Can you believe that?! I was a captive! My throat was constricting! My body burned. I wanted to run as fast as my legs could take me but for some odd reason, my body stayed put. I *owed* her? For *what?* For saving the life that I didn't want to have in the first place? For forcing me to continue to live in a loveless, joyless, meaningless existence that was doomed to fail miserably again and again? I was incensed to say the least, but I have to admit there was a part of me that was exhausted just thinking of trying to kill myself again.

"Go ahead then. Call the police. I really don't care," I said, surprising even myself.

"Ruby," said Blondell. "Go head an call de po-lease! Chile ain got no sense."

I stood there, paralyzed by the sound of the telephone being dialed. Everything flashed in front of my eyes—police cars, straightjackets, the whole works.

"Jail food gwine kill you if you don' do it firs'." I turned to face her and Blondell stared me down. Why something so simple as a sentence of bad jail food got through to me, I'll never know, but in that moment I made a conscious decision *not* to run. At least not yet. I'd wait awhile since I had no where else to go. What did I possibly have to lose? So I firmed my shoulders and straightened my jaw and said, "Yes, Miss Blondell. You saved my life, so I will do this—for you—but only for a little while."

Miss Blondell, grinning for the first time, displayed a big mouthful of white teeth and gold caps. "Das all I ax, chile," she said, nodding. "Das all I ax."

3

Summer 1948

Duchess

The first time I met Miss Blondell I was seven years old, just a little thing, when I wandered out to that big ol' empty clearing by the marsh of St. Anne's. Mama and Daddy gave me the run of the island back then, mostly to get me out of their hair, but I loved it. Freedom.

There she was, picking weeds, her skin black as licorice. Blondell stood straight when she saw me, her hands full of long, green sprigs. There was a dirty bag draped over her shoulder stuffed with more of the same.

She wasn't old back then, only thirty or so, but to a little girl she seemed old, you know. She's always seemed old. I stared at her. I'd never seen a woman so tall or so black. Or so scary.

"What'ya say now, chile?" she said. "Where yo' mammy?"

She put her hand on her hip, and I couldn't speak. I just clenched my hands, wondering if I should run.

"Gw'on now, shoo. Ah'z busy. Ain no time fa fool roun'." She bent down and pulled another weed up. I didn't budge. "Well ef you gwine stay ya, make use ob ya'sef. Come ya! Pick um up. Like disya. See?"

She stooped and pointed to a weed by my feet. I looked around and saw nobody—Mama was too far to holler—so I just did what she said. I bent down and pulled that weed. Then I did it again and again, and I liked it. It was a game now. Blondell would point. I'd pull the weed and stuff it in her bag. I was part of something—she was letting me help—something at that age I'd wanted desperately to do. And though she didn't say much more after that, I recognized an ally in Miss Blondell that very first day.

Throughout that summer and the ones after, I met Blondell and some island kids, black mostly, in the field for more pulling. She never had any children of her own as far as I know, but Blondell lured us back day after day with three-inch pieces of sugar cane, cut fresh. We'd flock around like she was the Pied Piper or some such.

To this day, I can taste the sweetness of those summers, though I had no idea then what Blondell was doing with those weeds we pulled. I still can't say for sure, though I've heard the rumors. All I know is—her being a root doctor and all—my back-breaking work went toward things more powerful than I could ever imagine.

July 14, 2006

Honor

Blondell proved to be a woman of her word. She did not call the police on me. To be honest, I couldn't bear it if she had. I would never have taken well to being under constant surveillance and psychological probing. Instead, she had Ruby walk me across the street. As promised, we were going to see "the Duchess."

We passed home after dilapidated home. I looked into each and every one, nodding at elderly people rocking on front porches and wondering which place would serve as my halfway house. After a while, the scenery changed. The streets became paved and lined in grand oaks, the branches forming a luxurious canopy overhead. The houses were larger, more regal. I recognized this place. I'd walked here many times, imagining what it would be like to live in one of these homes. Were they all as happy inside as they appeared to be from the curb?

Ruby talked the entire time although I cannot tell you about what. I was trying to make sense of everything—the surrealism of it all. Within twenty-four hours, I'd been kicked out of my home, attempted to kill myself, was saved by a band of three ıl black women, and now here I was, strolling in a ,аоulous neighborhood of the wealthy. The funny thing was, this is exactly why I'd come to St. Anne's in the first place—to become one of these people. To masquerade as them long enough so that the feathers and sequins would actually meld into my skin and transform me. But being here now, I felt as black as Ruby in this pristine white place. I simply did not fit in.

"We goin' right there," Ruby said, straightening her shirt col- lar. I lifted the basket of goodies Blondell had given me and stared wide-eyed at the house.

"This is where the Duchess lives?" I asked. It was not a house, it was a mansion. And pink. Antacid pink. There were white ionic columns, four of them, shouldering a hefty second floor balcony. I squinted into the morning sunshine. There was an incredible warm breeze blowing on my cheeks and through my hair. The ocean, in its splendor, was this woman's backyard.

"She been here a long time, 'round when her husband passed. *He* was a nice enough fella." Ruby said the word "he" as if "she" were not so nice.

"Is she really a Duchess?" It sounded so silly, but I had to know who I was dealing with.

Ruby laughed, and then cackled in a high-pitched screech. She wound up slapping her knees and trying to catch her breath.

"The Duchess? You thank Duchess a real Duchess? Lawd have mercy, that's the funniest thang I heard in a long time." Then she straightened back up and took my hand in hers, pulling me toward the door. "Miss Honor, the Duchess ain't no more real Duchess than me. We just call her Duchess 'cause she thank she royal. Her husband—he was a old, old man—he was a congressman or mayor or some such from out west. Some reason, Duchess thank the world owe her. Thank she owns everythang and everybody. You'll see. Just come on. Duchess, my behind," she said.

As we began climbing the rounded stairway, I noticed there was a thick film of mildew slathered across the stucco. I looked down at the flowers below—they were overcome with weeds. A pit grew in my stomach, and I wondered if the bacon Blondell had fed me had really been okay to eat.

When we stood at her front door, I looked over at Ruby. "Is she going to mind my staying here?" I couldn't understand why in the world someone would bring in a perfect stranger, but before she could answer, the door swung wide. Ruby and I both gasped.

Duchess

No, Honor couldn't for the life of her understand why someone would bring in a perfect stranger. And not everybody would, I can assure you. But I would 'cause that's just the kind of person I am. Southern hospitality, mind you. There's something to be said for it.

And yes, I know they call me "the Duchess." They do it to poke fun at me, but really and truly I don't mind. 'Cause part of it is true. When I first came back to the island, I was an insufferable old bird having lived under the care of my late husband. But I'm working on it. Really and truly I am.

When I opened that door, Ruby and Honor were standing there, mouths dropped wide open.

"Sonny? Oh, it's you," I said, disappointed. I stood there wearing my fur stole around my shoulders. And let me tell you, that's *all* I was wearing. My pale white skin was puffed and droopy, and I knew it full well. My breasts were most likely the largest Honor'd ever met in person. I showed no shame, no embarrassment whatsoever. And why should I? Honor was mortified though, I could tell, even though *she* was the one wearing sequins before ten in the morning. Gracious! She turned her head and stared hard across the street.

"Where your clothes, girl? Cain't be struttin' naked. Good Lawd! And what the world you got on your lip?" Ruby pushed in the door and dragged Honor in after her. "Come on, Duchess, let's find you somethin' to wear. Cain't nobody be runnin' 'round naked all the time!"

I grinned, my mustache-removin' cream rising into my nose as we left Honor standing in the oversized foyer. I pictured her watching my bare behind, poor thing, as I swaggered away. Like watching a terrible car accident. You know you shouldn't stare, but for some reason, you just have to. Honor told me later she wanted to flee for her life, and she eyeballed the doorknob, weighing her options.

Not sure why, but she stayed in the same spot 'til we got back.

I had wiped off my mustache, and I was still wearing my fur but had a long tan shift under it. I'd accessorized, too, with pink feathered slippers and a ball cap to match.

You know, I *was* attractive at one time. My features are small and refined, my eyes pale blue-gray. But dad-gummit, my hair shoots out in unruly white sprigs around my face, uneven because I cut it myself. I have to. Just can't bring myself to pay somebody to do it.

"Why, hey there, hey there!" I said, taking Honor's hands in mine. "Where are my manners? It's so nice to meet you. Are you a Peabody?"

She shook her head.

"A Jackson? Oh, you're one of the Abernathys, aren't you? Aren't you! Oh yes, I can see the resemblance—such strong cheekbones!"

"I'm sorry, no. I'm . . . Honor. No one you would know, I'm afraid." She looked over at Ruby for help.

"This is Miss Honor. Miss Blondell wants her to stay here with you awhile—you know—to help with thangs."

My eyes widened and I took a step closer. Then I walked around her in a circle, surveying her like property while the feathers on my cap tickled her ear. Her hair was shoulder-length, shiny but thinning, crisp on the blonde ends from over-dying. And her complexion was sallow and faintly pockmarked though she was still quite pretty with the most striking green eyes, almond-shaped like a cat's. Her lips were thin and her body was on the lean side, but her cheekbones were strong, and she held her shoulders back nice and tall. "Yes, yes. You will do fine. It is so hard to find good help these days. And I am so busy. So, so busy. You just would not believe how busy I am!"

Honor glared at Ruby.

"Yes! Welcome, my dear," I told her. "We're gonna become the best of friends! I just know it. Mark my words."

I smiled at her sweet as I could, then twirled on my toes and beckoned for her. "Wait here just one more minute, and I'll show you to your room."

I ran on up the stairs fast as I could and got the place ready for her—moved things around, put things away. Then I came back panting, trying to catch my breath. "Well, come on. Come on now!"

Honor took a step toward me and then looked back for Ruby. The front door clicked when it shut. Her green eyes were screaming, *She left me! With this crazy woman!*

Crazy woman. Hmmph. She'd just tried to kill herself, 'course I didn't know it at the time. But I was the crazy woman? Hmmph. Maybe I was the sane one.

With her tail between her legs, Honor followed me like I was pulling her from room to room on a chain. I told her all about the place and gave her a list of things she could help me with, but Honor didn't pay me no attention. She seemed distracted by my lovely décor—a mishmash of old Victorian pieces and oriental rugs—relics of my wealthy in-laws.

I noticed then, with someone else in the house, the short white hairs covering every square inch, and I was ashamed. Funny how sometimes you can't see things 'cept through other folks' eyes. Honor scratched her nose, and I hoped she wasn't allergic. She looked around nervously.

"Here we are, not much farther," I said. I led Honor to a sliding glass door facing the ocean. It was open wide, accounting for the dampness in the air. We walked through to the balcony covered in sunning furniture, and I noticed my plants were dead. That shamed me too.

"Oh, how nice," Honor said, eyeing the breakers rolling to shore. She pressed up against the railing and inhaled the salty air like her life depended on it.

"Don't do that!"

I grabbed her wrist and she froze, backing up a step.

"Oh dear no, that rail won't hold. There's a loose nail or board or somethin'. I keep tryin' to get Sonny to come up and fix it 'fore I plunge to my unsightly death down there." I looked over at the beach and shuddered.

"Sonny?"

"Yes, Sonny. He's my strappin' young houseboy—'course he would be mine if he'd ever let me get my hands on him. Oh, Sonny, Sonny, *Sonny*! That boy has a stomach so tight, why, I'd have my breakfast on it every mornin' if I could. Anyway, you might want to hold off on leanin' against that rail for now. Just to be safe."

Honor clutched her chest and followed me along the back balcony, stepping over things until we came to another sliding glass door. "This'll be your room," I told her, ceremoniously sweeping my hand to the latch. "It was my dearly departed husband's room—when he was alive, of course. I haven't been in here much since then." I fiddled with the latch.

"Must be a little rusty, but you got to come in this way. I had the other door boarded up to keep his memory from gettin' to me. That didn't work very well, I can assure you," I said, turning to face her, "so don't ever try it if you need to dispose of a particularly sticky memory. They have ways of seepin' through the cracks."

"I . . . I'm sorry for your loss," Honor said.

"Sorry? Oh no, dear. Don't be sorry," I assured her, crossing my arms. "He was a fool. I only married him because I thought he could bring me happiness. He was wealthy. Old money. He had power, you know. And there I was, young and beautiful, and I just happened to be looking for a wealthy, powerful man. It all worked out in the end, I suppose. I'm livin'. He's dead. The end. Ah ha!"

The latch finally gave, and I pulled the door to the side. The smell of mothballs struck us first. Honor's face flushed and she turned her head, gasping. I just wrinkled my nose. The room was dark and covered in plastic without a speck of fabric, carpet or otherwise showing. Our feet made crinkly noises when we walked across the floor.

"It needs a bit of fixin' up," I admitted. "What I need you to do is just run on out and get some cleanin' supplies. Windex, some carpet cleaner, maybe some ammonia. Ammonia always seems to work. Oh, and while you're there, can you pick up a little paintbrush? There's some touchin' up I need to do—in the kitchen mostly. That should do it for now, but please, make yourself at home. Be my guest, be my guest!"

I raised my arms in the air and surveyed the room, then felt the need to be doing something else—what, I have no earthly idea. But away I went to give my new houseguest some peace.

Honor

I was so glad when the Duchess had gone. Seagulls were crying outside, and the ocean brewed up against the shoreline just below me. I noticed the door to the bedroom—it was boarded up from top to bottom. If it weren't for the ocean air blowing in, I thought I just might suffocate.

Where am I? How did I get here? This is just great, Honor. You've really done a number this time.

I began peeling back the plastic from the bed, slowly at first. Then I moved to the other pieces of furniture, a mahogany dresser and writing desk, a full-length mirror and bookshelves. In frenzy toward the end, I ripped up the plastic on the floor and discovered the most gorgeous silk rug I'd ever seen with brilliant greens and purples and reds.

Once the plastic was gone and the room was exposed, I realized it had been preserved perfectly. It was a time capsule and most likely just as lovely as when the house was new. I felt like I'd found a quaint bed and breakfast on the Maine shore or the Potomac. In spite of myself, I felt a glimmer of—joy? Excitement? I can't tell you exactly what it was, but for the first time since I'd found myself alive, I thought there may be something here worth enduring.

Duchess

When Honor met me, I was a mess. I'm not proud of it. You ever get to the point where you got to keep busy, moving, shaking your foot, humming, whatever, just to keep a cotton-pickin' thought from blooming? I couldn't even allow myself to think, 'less I "think" myself six feet under. That's how bad I was then.

And you have no idea how hard it was for me to take Honor to that room where my husband used to sleep. It was like taking a can opener and popping the lid off the smelly can of tuna fish that was my life before.

My husband had been a powerful man. Or so I thought. He was old as the hills, even when I met him at age eighteen. He was fifty-two. I was a beauty, and he took notice. But don't think I didn't take notice of the life I thought he could give me. I was a country bumpkin and my daddy was poor as a dormouse. He never amounted to anything much. But then there was Mackey, dapper and rich, a man's man, getting things done. I liked the looks of it all, wrinkles or none. And I let Mackey raise me the rest of the way. I became a woman under his care, his little Missus, his darling trophy of a wife. He had folks doing things for me day and night and keeping me busy so I couldn't be bothering him. Taking up his precious time.

By the day Mackey died, I didn't know who in the world I was. I simply didn't exist anymore. I wasn't beautiful. I wasn't the wife of a powerful man. I was a nobody. And I didn't know how to be a nobody. And what was worse, I had no one to take care of my pitiful useless self anymore. And I hadn't the foggiest idea what to do from there.

Yes ma'am, that's why I tell you now, when Honor popped into my life, she was like a floating lifesaver sent from above to haul my flabby white rear back up on shore again. And going back into Mackey's room, into the stench of my previous life, was what I needed to do then. See, stink might can be covered up, but it doesn't ever go away unless it's aired out proper. That's something my mama could have told me, I suppose, had she been there that day instead of Honor.

4

Alice

The day my world stops is a Monday. It's two weeks before Christmas, and I'm driving when it happens—on my way to the grocery store. I'm wearing a red sweater and blue jeans and a silly toboggan with a ball on top—my oldest daughter made it for me years ago, and the weather's been unseasonably cool for December in the South. We've actually had snow for two days, though it turns to mud the second it touches the earth.

Snow in Murrells Inlet means hell has frozen over. Not that the place is hellish—it's lovely really, all four miles of it—but snow is a holiday that comes once in a blue moon. It's so rare that when we were growing up, my sister and I never touched a snowball and never made snow angels, if you can imagine such a thing. Instead we made sandcastles on nearby beaches year-round, and we made our angels in fluffy sand dunes, surrounded by desert flowers and sea oats waving gently in the breeze. Honor and I would lay down in hundred-degree weather. The sand would burn our skin until we burrowed down deep enough to feel the coolness of Colorado pressing into our backs.

On this day in Murrells Inlet, it's 28 degrees with a light flurry. Schools have closed, meetings are cancelled, and anyone in her right mind has stayed home for fear of snow-driving virgins.

My house is almost ready for company. My sister will be visiting from St. Anne's Isle, and my girls are coming home for Christmas break. My youngest has only been in college for one semester and already the emptiness has swallowed me whole. Even though Wayne is with me in our big house—perhaps *because* he's with me, the loneliness is impossible to bear.

I've just turned left onto Highway 17. There's a station wagon crawling in front of me, but for some reason, I don't mind. Instead I take the time to watch the white sky, how everything looks faded and washed out. To me, it's beautiful. And like the flashing taillights in front of me, I focus on the bright spots in my life: the people who matter most to me are coming *home*.

I'm about to break into a full-out smile—something I haven't done in a long while—when the car in front of me slams on its brakes.

There is nothing I can do.

I try to stop, but I plow into the back. Tires squeal, metal bends, glass shatters. The bones in my foot crunch, my neck jerks forward, and the seatbelt pinches my chest. My purse flies to the floorboards, sprawling lipstick and compact and—

I think I may have cursed. I don't know for sure.

A second later, an irate man is knocking on my window. What's he saying? He's round and balding and his eyebrows seem permanently pressed together as he yells obscenities at me. My mind is swimming, and I can't focus. I hear Beethoven far off in the distance, then I realize it's just my cell phone, singing to me from the floor like Odysseus' sirens.

For some reason, I let that awful man keep pounding on my window and choose to pick up the phone instead. Ten seconds later, I would do anything if I could just go back in time and un-answer it.

"*Hello?*"

"Is this Alice Chandler?"

"Yes."

"This is the Waccamaw Hospital. We have your sister here."

"Honor is there?" I can't comprehend it. She's not due in town for another few days.

"She's . . . it's pretty serious. Could you come on over?"

"What? Serious? Oh, I—yes! I'll be right there!"

I hang up and look around me. The angry man is still outside my window. I open the door and stare at him and the wreckage in front of us. Police cars are pulling over to the side of the road. I'm not fully aware of much more after this because the world is slowing down like molasses around me. And I'm frantic. Between exchanging insurance cards, calling a tow truck, and asking a policeman to take me to the hospital, the details slosh together like the mud around my feet.

I know Wayne will flip out when he hears I've wrecked the car, so I don't call him. It feels like one of those trivial things I can just keep from him like the extra fifty dollars I sent Sarah or the C Melody got in Biology. Even though I know at some point I'll have to confess, I have bigger problems to deal with. Something is terribly wrong with my baby sister.

Something is terribly wrong with my world.

I just know my foot's broken. I slammed on the brake too hard. At the hospital, the policeman helps me out of the car and lets me lean on him before settling me down in a wheelchair. I smell the staleness of his uniform and feel the heat of his arm around me. It's strange, feeling the skin of another man—other than my husband. It doesn't repulse me. That, in and of itself, is a shock.

He begins wheeling me toward the front desk.

"She needs to be looked at," he tells a lady I can only see from the chest up. "Her foot's broke."

"No," I say. "I can't right now, I've got to see my sister. Honor Maddox. What room is she in?"

The woman behind the desk looks confused. "Here. Fill this out." She hands me a clipboard.

"I can't! I need to see my sister. Honor. Maddox. *Please*, what room is she in?"

"You really need to have that looked at," says the officer.

"What room!"

"Uh, 221. The elevators are down that way."

I clutch the wheels and start pushing as hard as I can. My foot is throbbing. I back into the elevator door and yelp when I knock my foot. I'm fighting back tears when the policeman runs over and quietly escorts me up. I'm so grateful for his silence.

On the second floor, he insists on pushing me the rest of the way, and we find room 221 and part ways. Then I hold my breath, knock, and open the door slowly. Nothing could have prepared me for what I see in there.

My sister is lying in the hospital bed in a pale green gown, her head slightly elevated. She must have lost thirty pounds since I've seen her last and her hair is chopped short. It's always been long and silky brown. Her cheeks are gaunt and her skin pasty. In full alarm, I wheel to her side and grab her hand. It's completely still, bony. She doesn't look at me. "Honor? I'm here. It's Alice."

She doesn't respond.

"Honor? Honey, I'm here. Wake up."

Just then a woman in scrubs walks in behind me. "Are you Alice?"

"Yes! What's wrong with her?"

Honor is hooked up to machines with tubes coming in and out of her bed sheets. Red numbers register her heart rate and oxygen level.

The woman sits down to face me, and the wheels of her chair make rolling noises across the hard floor. I can see that her name is Sadie by the tag perched on her large bosom.

"I was hoping the doctor would be here by now," she says. "I reckon I got to be the one to tell you this." The woman glances over at Honor and closes her dark eyes. "Your sister has cancer." When she speaks those words, her gold loop earrings sway back and forth, and I want to vomit.

"Cancer?" I shake my head. "I—I don't understand. What kind of cancer? We don't have cancer in our family. I don't know how—oh, *please God, no.*" I run my hand along Honor's leg and feel how thin it is. "How far along is it?" I manage in a whisper, trying to stay composed for Honor's sake.

Nurse Sadie swallows uncomfortably and my stomach seizes up like a stone. Then her dark brown eyes change, weaken, and she smiles a very sad smile that she must think will soften the blow. "Miss Honor is very sick. She's got stage four breast cancer. It spread to her lungs, her liver, her brain. I'm real sorry."

"Stage four? I don't understand. How many stages are there?"

"Four," she says.

My head drops to my chest, shaking. "What? No! This can't be—how did this happen? Isn't there something we can do? Chemotherapy? Can we try chemo or something?"

"Far as I know, we've done as much as we can do," she says with finality. "Miss Honor's been here with us for three weeks."

My hand goes up to my mouth and I hold it there, afraid that if I move it a millimeter I'll scream bloody murder. Tears sting my eyelids and I let them fall, one at a time. *She's been here for three weeks? Why didn't she call me? Why didn't I know this? I'm her sister! How could I not know she was sick?*

My head trembles, this time in anger. "Why didn't you *call* me? I live here! I could have *been* here!"

"I'm sorry, but she asked us not to." It pierces me like a knife and I gasp, suddenly aware of the pain in my foot again. My tears come uncontrollably then.

I stare at Honor lying helpless on that bed. I hear wailing from my lips and the sound scares me. Words can't describe what it feels like to find my baby sister this way. I want to crawl under a bus and die myself. But what's worse is realizing that she's been here for three weeks without telling me. I've gone about my normal life—cleaning the house, planning my holiday menu like Martha Stewart—while she's been here, dealing with *this*. Alone.

"Oh, honey," I say softly, pulling her hand up to my lips. I want so badly to hug her, to kiss her face, but my wheelchair won't let me. "I love you, Honor," I tell her. "Oh honey, I love you. You're going to be okay. You hear me? You're going to be just fine." As soon as I say those words, I know I'm lying. So I gather my breath and I say them to her—one more time.

5

St. Anne's Isle
July 17, 2006

Honor

Do you remember when we were little girls, and we lived near that big cemetery? We had absolutely no fear of it. In fact, we'd stroll along the gravestones searching for ones with our first names on them. You'd lie down at every "Alice" and I at every "Honor," not that there were but a couple. We wondered about the lives those people led. Our heads on the cool earth, we'd watch the clouds stream above us, the trees blowing overhead. And we grieved a little for the people beneath. We tried to be a little reverent at least.

Well, I felt that way the first night I slept at the Duchess' house. Lying in her deceased husband's bed, I wondered about him. Mind you, I'd scrubbed the sheets clean and everything else in the room. I'd made it my own and was a little surprised at how I took to it so quickly.

My tendency in those first days was to keep to myself—locked behind that boarded door. I had a basket of food Blondell had sent with me, and I know it was rude not to emerge, but I simply couldn't help myself. There were times I felt like jumping off the balcony. At other times, I simply hid under the covers. I was safe and pensive there. But on the third day, I was ready to join the living. I decided to roam about the mansion and find Duchess. I was tired of myself and eager to hear someone else's story.

I found her sitting in the nude. The nude! Can you imagine? I had prepared myself, as much as one can be prepared for such a sight. She was sunning in a little courtyard with complete privacy except to the ocean. Her face was slathered in what appeared to be mud, and there were specks of ground shells dotting her cheeks. She didn't stir when I came to her side, and I found myself in the most awkward place possible. *Should I say something to her and possibly wake her up or should I slink away unnoticed? And if I do slink away, will she have known I was here and think I was watching her like some circus sideshow?*

Duchess

Honor was a few feet away from me, not saying a word. I was wearing nothing but pluff mud on my face. That's my beauty secret—pure pluff mud. Mama taught me that. I kept my eyes closed, wondering if Honor might talk, and when she didn't it turned strange. So I broke the silence.

"There you are," I said, not moving or opening my eyes. "I was wonderin' if you were all right. I would have checked on you myself, but I figured I'd wait for Sonny to come by. If you were dead in there, that's the last thing I wanted to find."

"I suppose they told you then," Honor said.

"Oh yes, they told me. Blondell sure was hot to trot. Don't get her started on the value of a human life."

"I truly did not mean to bother—"

"No bother! It's what they do—what Blondell thrives on. She helps people. She pretty much saved me, you know."

"I've heard that about her—quite a bit."

"No really, it's true," I said, sitting up and adjusting my eyes to the sunshine. I was painfully aware of my rolls enlarging and everything sagging, becoming more pronounced. Honor couldn't look but gazed off at the water instead.

"Can I ask you something?" She breathed in, gathering her nerve. "Are you . . . that way"—she gestured toward my body—"*all* the time?"

"What way, dear?" I teased.

Her face flushed. "You know . . . without clothes, I mean."

"You mean naked as a jaybird? Bare as a baby's bottom? Yes, mostly," I told her, turning serious. "Unless it's cold. I hate the cold. That's why we came back here in the first place. I used to spend my summers here as a little girl."

Honor sat down in the Adirondack chair and looked out at the ocean, waiting for me to go on. I really didn't want to, so she started small talking. "Your husband was in politics?"

"Oh yes. Mackey was mayor of Muldoon, Idaho. He was a marvelous pontificator. The public just adored him." At this, I stood up, arms swaying this way and that from my days of being in beauty pageants. "And me. They loved me almost as much. I was the first lady of sorts, and since I married him at such an early age, I suppose the public just enjoyed watchin' me blossom into the flower of a gracious woman." I stretched my arms overhead, spreading out my petals. "I was one, you know. Very gracious. And proper. One must be proper at all times in the public eye."

I flashed my eyes at her from behind the caked mud, and all of a sudden, I realized I was naked. Not that I have a problem with it, but in that moment, I just didn't feel right. Silly all of a sudden. "Let me just go put some clothes on, dear. Would you care for some iced tea? I'd love some. If you wouldn't mind grabbin' a couple of glasses—that would be super!"

I left, feeling like the empress with no clothes on, and Honor searched around for a pitcher of iced tea. Not seeing one, she headed into the house to find the kitchen. She told me later she literally had to catch her breath at the sight of it all. And I'm not proud of it. I'm not. But that's how it was then, no lie.

Honor

The sink was piled with dishes, none of them clean. There was an odor, a pungent sourness in the air. I nearly gagged. Her appliances, white, were filthy. There were cartons of milk left lying on the countertops. Mold was growing on everything. It was too much to handle! Every synapse in my head screamed in agony. I ran out the front door and stood on the drive, panting, gasping for air. I knew I wasn't sane enough to stay there any longer. Whatever sanity I had left in me was fleeing faster than I could.

I put my hand over my face and just stood there motionless. *Could I go? Where would I go?* I was free. I was still a free woman. I had no man, no children, and no life tying me down. I could simply run away and begin again. *Yes. I would begin again! I had done it before. So maybe it hadn't worked here on St. Anne's Isle the way I'd wanted it to, but perhaps it would work somewhere else.* I just knew it would. I simply hadn't found myself here. I'd bet money that the real me, the authentic me, was simply waiting to be found at the next place. *Where might that be? Savannah?* Oh yes, I always loved Savannah with its historic homes built around tailored squares. And it was on the water. It was perfect. I would find a way to get down to Savannah!

First, I needed to find my car.

I looked down both sides of the street, trying to get my bearings and determining the quickest route to the playground. It was then, when I looked to the right down a long row of oak trees, that I saw her. Blondell was standing tall, leaning slightly on a gnarled walking stick. She was stopped in the middle of the road, staring straight at me. *Had she walked all the way here for me? This hundred-year-old woman had hobbled here for me?!* Here I was planning my escape. The walls began closing in on me. I struggled to breathe but decided to compose myself. It would do absolutely no good to do otherwise. I raised my hand to her in a cordial greeting, "Well, hello. How are you doing?"

Blondell inched her stick forward and started toward me. I hurried over to her and met her in the road instead. I remembered when I was a little girl, I would see that look on Mama's face—you know, the one where her eyes grew so narrow they nearly crossed? I learned early that if I confessed to Mama what I'd done before she could bring it up to me, life would be a whole lot more pleasant.

"I'm so sorry I haven't come to the playground yet," I told her. "I've just been trying to recuperate. I'm feeling much better now."

Her brows nearly touched in the middle. "Come fa ya. Da meetin' oba ya."

"I know," I explained, "but I'm, well, I really don't think I'll be staying any longer. My sister, she's expecting me."

Blondell stepped closer to me, so close that I could nearly

smell what she'd had for breakfast. She studied me for the truth and I stiffened, trying to keep her gaze. At last, I knew she'd caught my lie. I faltered and looked down at my feet.

"Come ya. Ol' lady got bettah tings ta do." She turned around, leaving me stunned. I could do nothing else but follow her. It's hard to explain, but when this woman was around, whether it was her age or the way she carried herself, I was under her spell. She forced me to respect her. *Respect*. That's always been an issue with me.

I panicked at first but then realized she was taking me to the playground—exactly where I'd wanted to go in the first place! I was planning my escape. I'd humor Blondell and sit with the nannies for a while. Then I'd find my car and spin off south to Savannah, beginning my new authentic life. I just needed to be patient a little while longer. *Patience*. That's always been an issue with me too.

6

Honor

The playground of St. Anne's was a special place for me—a retreat back to my childhood. Palmetto trees lined it, waving up tall in the sky, and azaleas, when in bloom, painted green bushes pink and white. My favorite place to "play" was a hideaway made of bamboo that had been planted in a perfect circle. When no one was around, I would go in and stand there hidden by the foliage, listening to the leaves rustling, trying to calm my nerves. We felt safe there, the adult and the child in me, that is. But this day wasn't a day for solitude. Blondell had brought me there for serious business.

The swings were at full capacity. There was a child on every monkey bar, slide, and see-saw. They ran around, playing tag, boys chasing little girls and infants eating handfuls of earth in the sandbox. When Blondell and I walked up, none of the children batted an eyelash, but over at the nanny circle, it was a whole different story. Every woman, nearly a dozen African-American ladies, stood up from picnic tables and overturned trees and welcomed us with open arms. I was caught off guard, and my chest warmed with a brilliant glow. I knew that feeling. I'd felt it on occasion when Mama was proud of me or Daddy had said I looked pretty. And here I was, feeling that way again. I sat down on a log in front of the bamboo hideaway where they asked me to sit, and I smiled demurely. My desire to flee was temporarily on hold.

"Nice to see you," said Willa, folding her arms and rocking back. Her full cheeks spread into a smile. "How you holdin' up with the Duchess? She drivin' you crazy?"

"Oh no. She's very nice, actually. Very . . . interesting."

"She wearin' any clothes these days?" asked another graying woman, keeping one eye on a little white boy digging in the ground. "Last time I heard, Mister Calhoun said he won't deliver to her do' no mo'." She slapped her knee and belly-laughed. The little boy turned her way and grinned before picking up a toy truck.

The circle grew quiet all of a sudden. Blondell looked at me, so I returned her stare, feeling threatened. She seemed to be sizing me up, and I refused to look away. I tried my hardest to keep a steady glare without giving her the evil eye. Believe me, it was all I could do.

Then softness entered her face. Blondell appeared to be looking through me—into me. I shifted in my seat. She was scooping me out in little spoonfuls, and I was letting her. I needed her to sum me up.

A little girl came stumbling by us, breaking the tension. She was about four years old, with chopped blonde hair, straight and wispy. She was babbling something in between sobs. One of the younger nannies got up from her seat and grabbed the girl, holding her tight. "There, there, now," she said, swinging back and forth. Then she carried the girl off toward the water, pointing into the sky at pelicans dancing on the clouds.

Blondell tapped her walking cane against the log I was sitting on, jolting me. "Dey blessed, dem folks what ain got no hope in deyself. 'Cause God da rule oba dem."

She said each syllable with intensity, each word with the utmost importance. She was looking at me.

"Uh-huh. That right," said Willa. The nannies nodded and kicked at the dirt, keeping their eyes on their children. "Blessed are the poor in spirit," said Willa, "for they gonna see the kingdom of heaven one day."

The poor in spirit. That's me, I thought. *And I would have been in heaven right now if it weren't for you people.*

I recognized the phrase from the Bible somewhere, and my

mind flew back to Sunday school when we were little girls. Mama would force us to go. I'd tell her I didn't want to. We'd battle, fiercely. Then I'd throw up. It never failed. I'd win, spending the rest of my Sunday lying in bed and wondering which was worse, Sunday school or Mama taking care of me.

"Some people ain got no hope een deysef. Dey got ta look up. Look righ'ya," said Blondell, tapping her chest. "God up een ya."

Instinctively, I touched my chest like a child mimicking the adult and thought, *God's in here? There's nothing here but cobwebs and nightmares.* I reached up, pulling at my shirt collar for air. *My shirt!* No doubt, it belonged to one of these ladies sitting around me. I was wearing borrowed clothes from Blondell's basket. I was wearing borrowed clothes! I was an ant perched on a log. I itched to find my car, my belongings, and I turned my head toward the parking lot.

Blondell must have noticed my change in posture so she reached into her pocket. She pulled out a seashell and handed it to me, her knotted knuckles scraping my palm as she let it go. It was a small pink conch-like whelk shell that seemed buffed beyond what the sea can do.

"Give ta da Duchess," she said. I stared at it in my palm. I was leaving. Immediately, if not sooner. I was *not* going to see the Duchess. Ever! I was going to drive away from this place, away from these people and the failed memories of St. Anne's Isle and be done with it all. I certainly was not going back to that filthy madhouse on the ocean to see some naked debutante!

"Duchess need dis," said Blondell, emphatically.

"Oh yeah, she do," added Ruby in her squeaky voice. "She need that right now."

"Why?" I asked. "Why does she need a shell?"

"Got ta find out fa ya'self," said Blondell, pushing on her stick to stand up. "Look righ' ya, Miss On'ry. God up een ya." Blondell touched the hand still clutching my shirt, and apparently satisfied she'd voiced all she'd come to say, she turned from me and said her goodbyes. *That was it?* She strolled away, leaving me sinking in the sand.

The nannies turned away from me and began their chatter. "Chile, you won't believe what Mister Jones did this morning," said one to another. "Left his briefcase on the stove and that thing liked to catch on fire if I hadn't seen it!"

"Ain't that right. Got to have eyes in the back o' your head. Got to watch the children and the Mister and Missus both! Just last week—" The women cackled and grinned, each one sharing her story.

"I don't understand," I whispered to Ruby, pulling her aside from the party that was escalating around me.

"What's that?"

"I don't understand what I'm doing here. I don't understand anything about what just happened. What just happened?" I asked her, pleading.

"You had your first lesson, Miss Honor. It was a good one, if I say so myself. Miss Blondell, she the wisest woman I know," said

Ruby. Then she pushed my hand. "You go on back to Duchess and give her that shell now. You go on back and think about what Miss Blondell told you." She faced me and put her hands on the sides of my head, sending chills up my spine. "Pray for ears to hear with. Pray for eyes to see with. It's all there. Believe me." Then she pressed up on her tiptoes and kissed me on the cheek.

I sat down again, numb with the singing of children coursing through me, numb with the laughing and banter of the nannies, and hypnotized by the sound of waves rolling in. I loved St. Anne's Isle—even though I had nothing here—I loved it. It reminded me so much of home.

Murrells Inlet and the beaches nearby were unspoiled like this at one time. Remember how we'd spend the summers running along the water's edge, burying our toes, digging for sand fiddlers? We'd buy hushpuppies at that little fish stand in Seaside and dream of owning it one day. It would be the two of us, sisters in business, sisters doing life together.

But whatever happens to childhood dreams? Everything happens. For one thing, Alice, you got married and had a family. For another, I was no longer unspoiled like the crisp white beaches of yesteryear. I became tarnished along the way like one of those sad little creatures you see drowning after an oil spill. I was one of those poor little ducks whose feathers are stuck forever, poisoning him, killing him slowly.

After the nannies and everyone but a tourist family left the playground, I was left sitting, thinking about my life or lack of it.

I got up and burrowed slowly into the bamboo and breathed in the stillness. I looked up and saw a circle of blue sky. I opened my fist and looked at that stupid conch shell. There was no way I was staying with a naked woman any longer. The choice was clear: I had to go.

I marched through sand and mulch over to my green Jetta and peered into the window. Then I became frantic, trying to remember. "Where are my keys?" I pounded on the window. "Well, one doesn't need keys when one is killing oneself," I snipped. I could not believe this. My chance to start over again somewhere else, far away from anyone who knew what I had done, and this is what I get. I looked into the sky at God and felt His judgment on me. *This is your penance,* He was telling me. *Go serve your sentence.*

I'd been charged with a task, by Blondell and by God, and I don't know what it is about me—I hate letting people down, even though I did it so often. But I reasoned that it wasn't the end of the world. I would hand Duchess the silly shell, thank her for her Southern yet strange hospitality, and then call a locksmith to come and open the car door. And then I would begin my life— *my* life—whether I chose to live it or end it. It was mine.

When I got close enough to the Duchess' house, I saw the front door was open. I climbed the steps slowly, my feet dragging like lumps of coal. I was practicing my speech to her. *Get in and get out,* I kept telling myself. *Just go in, say goodbye, and then get the heck out of there.*

I stepped in the front door and heard a funny chirping sound. "Duchess? Are you in here?"

The noise stopped. "Yoo-hoo . . . hello. Anybody home?"

I didn't want to go in the kitchen, but I thought it was where I'd heard the noise. I walked through the arched doorway and saw her, sitting on the ground—that disgusting, dirty floor. The Duchess was crying, her shoulders shaking with sobs. I bent down and put my hand on her shoulder. She was wearing a blue terrycloth robe and sitting like a child on her knees.

Duchess

Trust me, I knew how pathetic I looked.

"Are you all right?" Honor asked me, knowing full well I wasn't. My face squished up, and I started boo-hooing again. I couldn't help it. There was filth all around me. I was a blue flower in soil, like I'd grown up out of it all. I pulled a pair of yellow rubber gloves out of the fold in my robe and then pointed to a bottle of ammonia by the stove.

"Were you cleaning? Are you trying to clean up?"

I nodded yes and grabbed her shirt, pulling her to me. I wasn't putting on a bit, I promise, but I wailed in her ear.

"Calm down now. Just calm down. I can't understand what's wrong with you." She took my hands and pried them away from her shirt.

"Can you take a deep breath now?" I did and tried to relax. I knew my face was puffy and red, and my nose was dripping. I swiped at it with the sleeve of my robe. I was an attractive woman at one point. I remember thinking then, *How in the world did it get this bad?*

"I tried to clean up for you," I told her. "I tried. I know you left me because of . . . all this." Tears poured down my cheeks.

"Oh no," Honor said. "No, I didn't. This? This is nothing."

I pointed to the dishes stacked up in the sink and screamed again like a banshee.

"Oh no, please don't cry. Look, we can have this cleaned up in no time. Here. Do you have another pair of gloves?" She looked around but didn't see any. I had the only pair. Honor seemed to be in much better shape than me, so I handed the gloves to her with a just-sucked-a-lemon look on my face. I knew it was a lot to ask. She'd probably go running *and* screaming this time.

"Would you do it?" I asked. "Would you clean this for me?"

Honor's eyebrows arched up.

"Please! I can't do it!" I screamed. "I just can't!"

"Oh, don't do that. Please stop crying. Look, I suppose I can," she said. Then to top it all off, she added, "Why don't you just go clean up. Go wash your face. I'll take care of it . . . somehow."

Can you *believe* that? What a sweet girl. After I left the room, I came back around and peeked in, watching. Honor stood up, surveying the damage, shaking her head. "Get in and get out. Get in and get out!" she kept muttering.

The grime would be too much for anybody, I suppose. She covered her nose and gagged a couple times. And I almost ran in when I saw her eyeing my knives on the butcher block— probably thinking she could end her misery right then and there—but *no*! She couldn't die there! It was a pigsty! Even I would admit to that. Honor deserved better than that, didn't she? *Didn't she?* But now, she did say she'd clean it for me . . . oh, what to do, what to do . . .

Finally, she came up with something that, to this day, makes me crack up thinking about it. I kid you not, I watched as Honor reached up and unhooked her brassiere in the back. Yes, she did. She really did. Then she went up in her sleeves and pulled the thing out.

She tied that brassiere around her head forming a nice little mask over her nose and mouth, and I thought I'd die laughing. I had to tiptoe away to the back room just to get it all out. But then I came back calm and believe it or not, it worked. Honor's contraption helped her to clean that kitchen. And my heart just melted watching her do it. No matter what she thought of herself, the Honor I'd just witnessed had a heart of gold. A true heart of gold. Mind you, it took her the rest of the day, but when it was all done, amazing! She worked hard, scrubbing every single surface. My arms would have fallen plumb off! I've never been able to clean like that. And Mackey never let me forget about it, neither.

Well, I stayed out of her way. Not meaning any harm, but

Honor was doing such a fine job in there, I didn't want to mess her up. 'Course, I could also see something bigger was happening. Not only was my kitchen being cleaned, but I could see it on Honor's face—the fury seeping out of her pores, her demons being exorcised. Far be it from me to meddle in other folks' healing. Goodness gracious, far be it from me.

7

Murrells Inlet
August 1968

Alice

"You girls might wanna get out of the house for a while," Daddy warned us in a low monotone. Seemed that Mama was in one of her "moods." Just the slightest offense and her face would get to glowing red like she could blow at any second.

"Okay, Daddy," I told him. He didn't have to tell us twice.

When Honor and I were little girls, we could find magic in just about anything outdoors—in the steam that rose up after a hot summer rain, in the baby frogs that bounced up from the creek beds. There were adventures lurking behind green marsh grass and armies of fiddler crabs guarding pluff mud castles. My sister and I were just two years apart and as close as two people could be. We spent our days navigating the labyrinth of waterways near our home in Murrells Inlet. Our canoe and our spirits knew the creeks by heart, and we never once lost our way.

Honor and I pushed off in our canoe and paddled with the wind behind us, sun glittering off the water, quiet mystery pulling us on. I remember stopping after a while. We'd been searching for treasure and I, the elder at age ten, was sure I'd seen a mound of gold hidden in the marsh grass.

Honor was so excited she jumped out of the boat first. She squealed when her foot hit the sticky pluff mud, the tar-like treasure of the Lowcountry that smells of rotten eggs and sunshine and home, and I'll never forget the look on her face when she realized she was sinking in it.

"Alice, I'm stuck!" she shouted before falling back. "Get me out!"

My mound of gold was nothing but a cluster of razor-sharp oysters—Honor was surrounded by them. Her shoes had been sucked down in the ground and Honor panicked, trying to pull her feet out. I grabbed her slick hand and pulled, but the boat kept slipping away. I needed to get my feet on solid ground, but there was no way to do that—without going into the mud myself.

"Wait here," I told her. "I gotta go get Daddy."

She looked at me helpless but knew it was the only way. She also knew Daddy'd be furious. Silently furious. He never raised his voice like Mother did. No, Daddy's kind of angry was even worse—as if you'd wounded him somehow. It was truly hard to bear.

I remember paddling until my arms burned. I don't know how long it took, but Daddy and I flew back in his johnboat as fast as we could. I just knew Honor had drowned in the rising tide, but when we got there, she was lying on her back, arms and legs spread eagle and stuck from head to toe. Her hair had completely disappeared, and there were only a few white spots of skin left on her as if the ground was swallowing her whole.

"Jiminy Cricket," Daddy swore under his breath.

"Hey, Daddy," Honor said innocently, grinning as big as she could, unable to lift her head.

Daddy pulled her out and washed her in the salty water, and while she was nursing her feet and arms, bleeding from the oyster shells, Honor whispered to me, triumphant.

"Is it pretty, Alice?"

"Is what pretty?"

"Right there." She pointed to the tracks she'd left in the mud. "I made an angel. See the wings there? See the wide skirt?"

And I did see it, although it was beginning to slosh back together. She was a lovely black angel. And it wouldn't be the last time my baby sister would make something beautiful out of a truly dark moment. That was one of her gifts. But it seemed for some reason, Honor would spend a lifetime working herself to death, trying to wash that black mud off her glowing angel skin.

There are some lives so tainted, there simply isn't enough water to do such a thing.

8

Honor

I had completely forgotten about the shell. My first thought when my eyes popped open the next morning was that conch shell Blondell had given me for the Duchess. I didn't want to give it to her if truth be told. I was still mad and amazed she'd finagled me into cleaning up her royal highness mess. However, I did wake slightly rejuvenated, knowing at least I could have coffee in the kitchen without contaminating myself.

My second thought was about you, Alice. I missed you! I wanted to hear your voice, and I knew by this time you'd be worried about me. You'd probably tried to call me for days. I hated that I was making you worry.

I decided calling you was more important than the Duchess' shell, so I wandered into the house to find a telephone. I found one, an old-timey thing, black with a dial instead of buttons, perched on a little stand in the study. I stared at the books around me, illuminated blue by the impending rain outside the window, then I dialed zero to speak with an operator.

Duchess

It's not like I was eavesdropping or anything. I'd just been minding my own business, coming out from the bedroom, but the library is just outside my door, you see. What was I to do?

"I'd like to make a collect call, please. Yes. Honor. Her sister, Honor."

I stood frozen for a second, then peeked in and saw Honor standing, twisting the cord around her finger.

"I'm okay, don't worry," I heard her say. "We just had a bad storm and the phone lines went down near my house. It might be awhile before I get connected again."

She lied very easily, I noticed.

"I'm sorry. Really."

Silence for a while. Her sister must have been jibber-jabbering.

"The mafia? That's crazy!" Honor laughed unconvincingly. "I'm not in trouble, Alice. And certainly not with the mafia. Well, yes, I did know some shady folks in Florida, but those were Brett's friends, not mine. You tell Sarah to just focus on school and stop worrying about her Aunt Honor, okay? Her dreams aren't always right, you know. Remember when she thought you were pregnant again?"

Honor snickered and turned my way, and I ducked against the wall, not breathing. It would be awful if she thought I was a snoop. I tiptoed closer to my bedroom door and stood like a statue. I could still hear her voice.

"Well, how are the girls?" she asked, sounding like she wanted to change the subject. "So what else is new?"

They chatted like that for an hour and let me tell you, my legs were getting tired, standing there. It was a most difficult predicament. I could walk on by, I supposed, but I just kept wondering when she might mention me. Imagine, not saying a word about the person you're staying with—the person who took you in—for an entire phone conversation. But she didn't. Not a cotton pickin' word. I could tell how much it meant for Honor to speak to her sister though.

"It's wonderful to hear your voice," she'd say, or, "Oh, I miss you. You sure you're doing all right?"

At times, she was gazing out the window. Other times, pacing the room, but the odd thing was I never heard Honor say one thing about her current circumstances. Just made everything sound hunky-dory and kept small talking till I thought I'd lose my mind.

"Oh no. I—well, I started to stop by the gallery, but there were so many people in there and . . . well, anyway. I'll go in and talk to them some other time. How about you? What are you reading right now? Anything good?"

Honor was quiet for a while, then sounded annoyed. "Just tell him we haven't talked in a while. . . Oh, Alice, please. He's a grown man. Tell him to make his own supper! . . . But I don't ever get to—no!" she said, "I mean, no, I'm—going out right now—shopping. So I'll call *you* later, okay? I'll just . . . don't worry about it. We'll talk tonight, all right? I'll call you. Tell Mr. Man I hope he enjoys his meatloaf."

Hanging up the telephone, she closed her eyes, fighting back tears. That's when I sprang into action and sneaked past the doorway. When I walked by, Honor didn't see me, but I could tell she was crying now. Her hands were over her face, and she was trembling, leaning against the bookshelf.

Honor finally came into the kitchen. My heart was settling down from rushing so, and I was trying to breathe in slow and natural. I was sitting at the table staring out over the sand dunes, clothed for once, in a floral smock. I realized it was the first time I'd been able to sit there without bugs crawling around me. How long had I lived this way? I didn't move when Honor first walked in. I heard her say "good morning," but I just sat frozen, staring.

"Are you all right?" she kept on.

"Oh, hello, Honor," I said, breaking free from my stupor and turning on the charm to show her everything was okay. "I was just enjoyin' this beautiful view. Isn't it lovely?"

"It is."

"I just love the colors we get before a storm." I breathed in deep and then slapped my knee. "Would you care for some breakfast?"

"Yes, that would be—"

"I don't think we have very much," I interrupted. "It would be nice if someone could go to the store. I just have so much to do this mornin', though. Would you mind runnin' out? Are you hungry?"

I bit my lip, waiting. *Breathe in, breathe out. She's not gonna do one more thing for you, you old cow!*

"Actually, I'm not that hungry," she quipped, no doubt lying through her teeth. Little stinker. I knew that child was hungry. "I think I'll just have some coffee," Honor said. "Mind if I make some?"

Honor

Ha! Two could play at this little game. I'd already seen the coffee the day before, and I knew for a fact the coffee maker was clean. Even though, officially, I *was* her houseguest and I owed her for that, I was not about to be treated as a hired hand. I just wasn't! I'd starve before I let that happen. No. Around this woman, I'd have to leave my guard up. She was so manipulative with her soft, lilting, pathetic voice (she sounded sick whenever she asked me to do something) and those forlorn eyes. Anyway, I was not going to be suckered again.

The Duchess sat quietly at the table while I brewed the coffee. After I talked myself down from my anger, I remembered the shell in my pocket. I wanted to be rid of it—the burden of carrying it.

"I saw Miss Blondell yesterday. She asked me to give you something." I walked to her and opened my hand. Duchess stared for the longest time. Then she took it from me, closed her fists around it, and turned toward the window again, sucking in air.

"Oh . . ." she whimpered.

I gave her a minute to elaborate, but she didn't speak. "Everything okay?" I asked.

She nodded, and then the tears came. Oh, terrific. I couldn't handle any more dramatics. The Duchess stood, waiting for me to console her, no doubt. When I didn't move or say a word, she started for the door, and I just let her go. I didn't know what to do. Obviously this shell had upset her, but I wasn't quite sure I wanted to know why. I'd asked about her crying yesterday and ended up with blisters on my hands from scrubbing her kitchen!

The back door shut quietly, and I heard her footsteps dropping, one by one, down the stairs. I know it sounds awful and ungrateful, but I was happy to be rid of her. I poured a dark cup of coffee and sipped it, my body growing more alive with every drop. I looked around at the kitchen—*very nice*. I thought to myself, *I could get used to a place like this.*

Peering out the window, I watched as the Duchess stumbled toward the dunes. She stopped and fell to her knees, shaking. Finally, I couldn't take anymore. I did have a heart—I needed to go out there and see what was wrong.

Barefoot, I followed a little walkway though sea grass and sand spurs, stopping now and again to curse and pull one out of my heel. The air was warm and fragrant like fresh baked bread, and sand billowed against my ankles as I made my way over to Duchess. Her peach-colored dress was blowing in the strengthening wind and her white hair danced around her head like Medusa's snakes. She was down on all fours but sat back on her knees when she sensed my presence.

There was a mound of shells in front of her—perhaps fifty of them, all different shapes and colors—sheltered from the sea by tall waving sea oats. She was still clutching the one I'd given her in her right hand, and she didn't look up at me.

"There's an old African belief that there are souls that lie in a realm beneath the waters—souls of African ancestors that were forced into Middle Passage. Seashells link these souls with their voices." She paused while lining her shells in rows, and then she messed them up again and formed a pile. "Blondell told me once that when Gullahs bury their dead, they cover the graves with seashells to give respect to the spirits of the waterways. By water they came and by water they'll return. The shells are a conduit to the spirits crossing back to the Motherland."

I was stunned, hearing her voice. It sounded completely different—low and genuine. There was an honesty I hadn't heard before. The Duchess opened her hand and rubbed the pink whelk shell. Then she raised it to her lips and kissed it. Finally she set it gingerly on top of the mound. Was this a grave? Her husband's?

"Did something happen out here?" I asked her.

She didn't speak, but her face turned dark beneath a passing cloud.

"I'm sorry to pry, I just—"

"Thirty-five years ago, Mackey and I were expectin' twins. We could not have been happier," she said, picking up a fallen sea oat and doodling in the sand. "He knew it was wonderful for his career to be a family man. For me, I was just tickled to death at the thought of bein' a mama . . . oh goodness, just so tickled . . ."

I knelt down in the sand beside her and stared at her altar of shells.

"They died at birth, both of 'em. They came too early. Back then, doctors couldn't do what they can do nowadays. They just didn't make it."

"My goodness, I'm so sorry. How terrible for you," I said.

She turned to me and smiled vacantly. "Thank you, dear." Then, facing the ocean and standing, Duchess released a fistful of sand into the air. We both watched as the breeze carried it away.

"I never was able to get pregnant again. So I have nobody now. No family, no children, no grandchildren. Miss Blondell knows me though—very well. She knows I need to let go all over again, every year 'bout this time. It's somethin' I just can't seem to get over."

Then she turned to me and said, "I don't think we ever truly get over somethin' like that, do we? It comes back to me again and again. The grief, I mean. The emptiness."

Her eyes welled and she added, "I think I'm going to take a walk on the beach now. I could stand to get my blood movin'. You want to join me?"

"No, I can't, I—"

"Sure you can. It's a beautiful mornin'. Storm won't be here for a good while yet."

"No, really, I have some things—"

"Things, Honor? What do you really have to do today, hmm?" she said, turning sour. "You need to try and kill yourself again? Is that it?"

"Excuse me?" My eyebrows rose.

"I know you still think about it, don't you, Honor. I bet you're thinkin' right this very second how you wish you could vanish off the face of this earth."

"You don't know anything about me." I turned away with every intention of leaving for good but then added, "And I am sorry about your loss, truly, but—"

"Which one do you want, dear?" Duchess interrupted me, pointing to her shells.

"I'm sorry?"

"Which shell do you want? Or we can go lookin' for another one right now—just for you."

"I don't understand."

"You've lost somethin'. You're grievin'. Why else would life get so bad that you don't want to live it anymore?"

I had no words. No one had ever cut right to the core of me so easily.

"You can leave now," she said, matter-of-factly. "I really don't mind. Not like I need you around, because I don't. I've done mighty fine on my own all these years. So go on now. Kill yourself for all I care, but I'm tellin' you right now, I've been there. Right where you are now. And there *is* life on the other side."

I stared down at my feet and watched as the sand polished my toes. Duchess stooped and rearranged her shells again silently. It hit me then. Somehow her mourning ritual had become all about *me*. Everything was about me, wasn't it? I was sick to death of me.

"Let's go," I told her. Duchess gave me a little smile, and we turned and walked toward the water. I wanted to go with Duchess, not because I felt sorry for her, not because I wanted to give her a shoulder to cry on, but because all of a sudden, she had churned up in me a stunning, aching misery that I thought I'd buried deep enough a long time ago. It began flooding back like the rising tide.

I hated to feel—to *truly* feel. I much preferred a state of numbness. So I needed to walk. And walk. And walk. I needed to find shells for my soul and pick up fistfuls of sand, and just . . . let it all fly.

*We were quiet for a while until we passed an aging light-*house and I spoke up. "My sister, Alice, and I spent our childhood walking like this, finding shells, swimming in the waterway, just doing whatever we pleased." I breathed in deep and let it out. "Just the smell of salt water sends me back."

"You miss her, don't you? Alice is very special to you, I can tell." Duchess placed her bare feet one in front of the other as if walking on a balance beam.

"I miss her more than you know. I'd do anything for Alice." I stopped and leaned down to pick up a broken sand dollar, fighting back tears. "She's truly the best person I've ever known. She's so good, like an angel." I brushed it off and stuck it in my pocket. "My sister is just a much better person than me. Than anyone. And she deserves so much better than what she got in a husband."

"First of all, I cannot imagine anyone being *better* than you." Duchess nudged my arm and winked at me. "No really, what's this fella like, her husband?"

"Wayne? Oh, he's not so good. Not for her, anyway. Put it this way, if I could have searched the world over for the one person I did not want her to marry, it would have been him."

"I'm so sorry, dear. It's terrible how we simply cannot take care of the ones we love the most in this world."

It was nice to be able to talk to Duchess. She seemed so normal then, walking past the jetty of barnacle-crusted rocks and minnows dancing in green pocket pools of water. Everything was so near the surface with me—just under my skin—and I thought if I could just get it all out, maybe it would be okay. If I could just tell her everything, this perfectly loony stranger . . .

For the first time in my life, I considered divulging to another human being my deepest, darkest secret. It's a secret I haven't even told you yet, Alice. I'm sorry, I will, I promise—just not quite yet.

Of course I didn't do it—open up to her, I mean. But the simple fact that it crossed my mind—that after an entire lifetime of secrecy I would imagine giving breath to those words—meant something was stirring in me. I did, however, tell Duchess one thing about me—something we very much shared in common.

"You know, I never had any children, either," I told her. "It's not that I didn't want to, it's just . . . it never happened for me. I made so many mistakes . . . with men . . . with everything. Anyway, I can't imagine what it feels like to lose your children—I don't pretend to know—but I do know what it's like to have a gnawing ache in your soul. Like a hole. Like something's missing, you know?"

Duchess wrapped her arm in mine then and we walked that way in silence, the pain between us palpable. I hoped my sharing could help Duchess not feel so alone anymore. Although I can't say it was completely for her sake. I know you always tried to listen to me and understand how I felt about not having children, Alice, but you have two beautiful girls to look after. You love them and they love you back. I have nothing. No one. You were always so sweet about it, but you can't possibly know how it feels.

So Duchess and I shared this sorrow, in different ways perhaps. But we were still two women who'd desperately wanted children, women who felt less than women because of it. We didn't have to say it—it was simply there like the air or the sea or the ground beneath our feet. We were both floundering and wondering what on earth we were here for. She didn't have the answers and, heaven knows, neither did I.

By the time we returned to the mansion, my feet were flat and aching, and my hair was a nest of sandy wind-blown curls. We hadn't settled anything between us, hadn't solved any of the world's problems, but our little confrontation and confession had done one thing for me—it let me know that Duchess wasn't quite as crazy as she seemed, and like it or not, she pretty much had my number now.

We washed our feet off, heated up some canned soup, and then I headed for the playground. It was nearly twelve noon and I could tell by the indigo sky that it was already raining on the mainland.

9

Honor

I went to the park, not because I was ready to hear what Miss Blondell had to say, but rather because I was thinking, wheels turning, and my feet needed to stay in motion in order to keep up with my mind. Not to mention, I now knew Duchess was in cahoots with Blondell, and she would've made me go whether I wanted to or not. I certainly didn't feel like taking her on again so soon.

Through palmetto trees I could see the storm clouds poised above the children's heads, eager to dump wet loads, but the children were oblivious, running, racing, laughing.

Ruby and Willa were there in sweatpants, smiling from ear to ear, and Blondell acknowledged me and nodded reverently. The other nannies' eyes were on their children, their faces serious.

"Boy, get your fool hide over here right now!" one of them yelled. A little boy with glasses was perched on top of the monkey bars and four or five other kids were under, taunting him. The largest kid pulled the boy's shoes off, and he retracted his feet to his chest as they grabbed for his legs. Finally, one kid jumped high enough to grab his clothes, and they all tugged at him until the boy and his glasses plummeted in a heap onto the ground. He wailed in pain and then tried to hold it in as the other kids laughed at him. That was all the nannies could take. They were waving their hands and moving in.

"Don't make me grab no switch now. G'won!" Willa yelled. The kids scattered like fiddler crabs in all directions. The nannies grabbed up their naughty children and a couple tended to the crying boy. I jumped to my feet, ready to help, but as soon as it had started, it was all over. The boy was all right, no broken bones, and he stopped crying soon enough. I just sat there, watching. My heart ached for that little boy, and I cursed the bullies who drove him to the ground.

Life is just full of bullies.

I sat down on a log across from Blondell and gave her a weary smile. "So how are you doing today, Miss Blondell?"

"Jus' fine fa a ol' lady. How Duchess?"

"Duchess? Oh, she's well, I suppose. I gave her that shell. It meant a lot to her. She told me all about her children and every-thing. It's very sad."

"Mm hmm." Blondell was eyeing me hard. I could tell she was searching me again, trying to read between my lines. The other nannies came back and sat. The bully kids were all sepa-rated now, each playing in solitude. The nannies were still mum-bling under their breaths when Blondell cleared her throat. She pounded her walking stick into the earth and lifted her finger. Her big lips spread as she pulled in air, preparing to speak words of wisdom.

"Watch oba ya heart real good," she said, slow as molasses, "fa een da heart eb'ry'ting een life gwine on. Miss On'ry, what'eba een yo heart gonna turn yo life eedah dis way or dat."

"That's what I'm sayin'," said Willa.

"Ain't that right?"

"Mm hmm." The nannies nodded their heads in full agree-ment. I, for one, hadn't understood a word. Although there were Gullahs in Murrells Inlet growing up, the Gullah language was nothing I was mastering easily. Ruby must have seen my eyes crossing, so she jumped in and squeaked her translation.

"What she said means, *Guard your heart above everythin' else, 'cause your heart determines the course o' your life.* It's from Prov-erbs, Miss Honor. You know Proverbs?" Yes, I knew Proverbs, not well, but I knew it anyway. Before I left, Blondell handed me a little white Bible and another to take back to the Duchess. I remembered them stacked up on her bedroom dresser.

I thanked her and the others, but honestly thought it was a complete waste of my time. I'd already learned years ago how to guard my heart. I'd guarded it like the pyramids in Egypt with magic so strong no one could come in. I'd done a lousy job of caring for my ex-husband, Jack, and I'd been pathetic in my care of you, Alice. I was unable to truly care for another living being, but my heart was the one thing I *had* tried to take care of all these years.

So that was my next lesson: *guard your heart.* Guard my heart. *Great advice—but a little too late,* I thought.

St. Anne's Isle
July 19, 2006

Duchess

Honor and I worked together the next morning to make a big breakfast, Southern style—it was gonna be delicious— steaming, buttery grits, fried ripe tomatoes, and flaky buttermilk biscuits. Mm-mmm. We started right after Honor's eyes bugged out at the sight of me, and I ran back to the bedroom and covered myself with a robe.

"Mama used to let me cook with her," I told her, tying my apron on. "Cookin' next to Mama was akin to bein' in heaven."

"Not for me," Honor said.

"No?"

"No. My mother fussed and fumed over every crumb, every drop of spilt milk."

"What a shame," I said, cracking my eggs into the bowl. "You know, I always dreamed of someday cookin' with a daughter of mine like Mama did me. I think that's what it's aaaa-ll about."

Honor seemed to have slipped somewhere out over the ocean, and the oil she was pouring into the frying pan dribbled instead onto the floor.

"Here, let me get that for you, sugar," I said, reaching down with a wet cloth. We caught each other's eyes and she apologized, tucking a strand of hair behind her ears. "Oh, look at me, never paying attention. No wonder Mama hated cooking with me."

"Now, hush. You know that's not right."

"Well, what's true is true," she said, dredging her sliced tomatoes into some flour, salt, and pepper, and then into the crackling oil. "Daddy didn't mind though. He was in charge of the grill. He always let me flip the burgers, and I never let them burn. Or if I did, he certainly never complained about it." Honor flipped the first round of tomatoes over, then she grabbed a wooden spoon and stirred the grits slowly. "I really did love that man, my daddy. Loved him more than Mama did. More than anybody, really, I bet. I would have done anything to please him. I tell you, if I could have married Daddy or somebody just like him, I would have. You think that's strange?"

"Why no, honey. That's not strange. It's just a little girl thing."

"Maybe," she said. "But I craved Daddy's attention. He didn't give it very often. I was just drawn to him—his quiet, his strength. Every morning before school I'd throw up because I didn't want to be separated from him."

"Oh, now honey."

"It's true! Sounds cuckoo, I know, but I idolized the man to a point I really don't think was healthy. I was like that as a child, always teetering on unbalanced. Alice was the good one, and I was the wild child. I wanted to scream from the rooftops, "*Look at me! Look right here!*" But girls just didn't do that back then—did we?—we were still life, quiet, behaved."

"You're tellin' me," I told her. "Try growin' up twenty years earlier. Talk about not makin' waves . . ."

"Yeah, but I *did* make waves. I bucked horns with Mama so often my head hurt. I've never told anyone this, but I'd actually pray at night for Mama and all her sternness to just go off and leave us there all alone with Daddy. How's that for unhealthy?"

"We all have our issues, dear."

"I suppose. The crazy part is, I actually miss Mother now. The one I wanted to be rid of most of all and now that she's gone, I feel cheated. I can hear her too. *Don't you mess with that boy, Honor. He's nothing but trouble! Or, Honor! You will not wear that dress tonight. People will think you're a regular harlot!*"

"That's mamas for you," I said.

"Yeah, mamas."

Just then, the most peculiar thing happened. A palmetto bug 'bout the size of New Hampshire buzzed right in front of us, scaring me half to death, and landed right smack dab on my clean countertop!

"Oh good gracious!" I screamed. "Here!" I threw my towel at Honor. "Kill it! Kill that thing!"

"No!" Honor said. "No." And she put her hands up in front of it in a protective sort of way.

"Well move, then. Let me at it!"

"You can't! It's bad karma! You can't kill an animal."

"That's no animal, that's a cockroach for heaven's sake, Honor! And it's about to eat my breakfast! Now move out of the way!"

I swatted at that nasty bug and it ran underneath my biscuit batter. "Oh no you don't! Don't you dare! Now come on outta there." I ran to grab some spray from under the cabinet and then chased that dirty thing onto the floor, spraying with everything I had in me till it was safely in the hallway and away from the food.

A few seconds later, Honor was standing next to me, and we were both watching that big ol' bug on its back, legs flailing, dying there with a trail of poison behind it.

"This is on your head," Honor said in a sullen voice. "Not mine."

"I'll handle bad karma any day," I told her. "But no bug's gonna mess up my breakfast. Now come on in here and let's eat finally."

"I'm not hungry," she said, just like that.

"What? Oh now, come on, Honor—"

"No, really. Please. I'm—I'm just going over to the playground a little early. You eat. Don't let it go to waste."

"Oh, honey," I said, futilely. My goodness, what a sensitive creature I was dealing with. And here I was, thinking we were doing so well.

Honor

*I lied to Duchess. I thought about going to the play-*ground, but instead I headed straight for the beach. I couldn't bear it any longer. I didn't think any of this was amusing anymore. I was not a child. I was forty-five years old, middle-aged, graying, yet for some reason, grown women felt they needed to raise me all over again. I tasted old bitterness rising up to my throat.

Your heart determines the course of your life. Yes. Of course it does. It was so simple. My heart, my impure, evil heart, was exactly the reason my life had gone so terribly wrong. There it is. That's the truth. And let me tell you, it's a painful pill to swallow. Duchess had lost her two children at no fault of her own. And me, I'd always liked blaming my problems on someone else. But when it came right down to it, I was the one who brought everything on—all of the strife and every bit of turmoil. Bad karma in its purest sense.

When I first moved to Florida, I was trying to start over. I was driving my big sister's hand-me-down BMW, and Brett got an eyeful—a pretty girl in a nice car. He assumed I had money, and

I didn't let him know otherwise. But then everything moved so quickly, and he was charming—back then, anyway. He used to buy and sell properties, and he swept me up into thinking there was a lot of money to be made. Then he had me cosign on all of his "deals."

I'm so embarrassed to say this because I always wanted to make believe I had created this nice little life for myself down there, but the truth is, I was broke and Brett was broke. Neither one of us had two dimes to rub together. He was faking it and so was I.

So after a couple years, all of our "deals" went sour. We couldn't pay our mortgages, and the IRS put a lien on our own house because we couldn't come up with $4,000. I was humiliated, but no, I didn't ask you and what's-his-name for the money because I'd gotten into that mess all on my own, thank you very much.

Alice, can I just tell you what it feels like to walk into a bank and not be able to open a simple checking account because your credit is so bad? Did you ever wonder why I only carried cash? Brett's credit was terrible before I met him, and then he destroyed mine. I had no idea all that could happen. I had no idea that a person could walk around like I did, feeling lower than human—feeling unworthy of looking a stranger in the eye. I cannot express to you the utter humiliation I felt then. And trust me, it only got worse.

But why, Honor? Why did you allow those things to happen? Why did you pretend you were someone you weren't and fall for a user like Brett? That's what you're asking right now. I know because on St. Anne's Isle, I thought of very little else. And the answers were there—I just wasn't ready to face them.

Please guard your heart, Alice.

Duchess

It was hard for me—knowing something was wrong with Honor, but not knowing the depths of it. At times it was like having a moody teenager in the house. Honor would skulk around, sighing when she thought I wasn't there. More than a few times I'd caught her out on the balcony with glassy eyes. "What's the matter?" I'd ask her. "If you can't tell a beautiful old Southern gal, now who can you tell?"

"Oh, it's just allergies. The pollen is giving me a fit," she'd lie. Else, she'd change the subject real quick.

Yes, I knew Honor was suffering something terrible. Over what, I did not know for sure. I thought it could be that old boyfriend of hers, yes, or maybe her ex-husband, but they were just men. From my vast years of experience, a woman can be irked to being uncivilized by a man, would like to pull her hair out or what's left of his, or possibly scratch the dickens out of his brand-new paint job—but to want to end her own life? Commit suicide over one? No. That's a desperation not every woman feels—only the woman whose grief burrows so deep she might never be able to reach it and pluck it out to be whole again.

I wondered, though, how long it might take for Honor to finally spill her beans to me. I hoped it wouldn't be too long. And I prayed she'd get over whatever it was mighty fast before she tried to up and kill herself again. I'd lie in bed at night terrified of it. Every sound I heard, I wondered if it was her. Trying it again.

Now most folks don't take me for a praying woman, but I'm never above getting down on my knees for someone I love. And I knew this much, I was growing attached to Honor, depressed or not. Heck, if it was a contest and I wanted to win bad enough, I could beat Honor at "depressed" any day of the week. Mark my words. She had nothing on *me*.

10

Waccamaw Memorial Hospital,
Murrells Inlet
December 11, 2006

Alice

My foot is indeed broken, three toes anyway. I'm x-rayed, put in a big blue open shoe, and given something for the pain, which is all right with me. I wish they'd give me even more. They ask me if I have someone who can take me home from the hospital, but I tell them flatly, "I'm not going home." Instead, I go back to Honor's room.

Seeing her again is a fresh shock. I'm on crutches now, and I hop over to her, lean the crutches up against her bed, and bend down. I hug her and want to squeeze her hard, but I feel instantly

94

how frail she's become. She's a shell of my sister. The Honor I know is vibrant and beautiful. She has a zest for living that I don't seem to have. She's the wild spirit that I live through—me in my tidy shoebox of a life.

We're alone for a while. I watch the numbers on her monitors change. Her breathing is very slow, and her chest hardly moves. There's a brown bandage around her chest, peeking out from beneath her gown. It's the same thing I wore after giving birth, trying to keep my breasts from becoming engorged. It makes her chest look flat. Honor's always had a full chest, something the boys loved and I envied.

I am unable to feel much of anything. I'm grateful for the sedative. I'm thinking of calling Wayne. He'll be worried about me by now. He'll be pitching a fit, cursing, and if he's been drinking, possibly throwing things if his dinner is not hot and waiting for him when he gets home.

I don't want to call him.

For a while, I just sit with arms and legs crossed, head cocked to the side, and eyes open, staring at Honor. I can hear feet shuffling across the cold, hard floor in the hallway. I'm not sure how, but life still seems to be going on around me, without me, circling in some far-off place. My spirit has floated away somewhere, leaving just a hint of me lingering here in the chair like a whiff of escaping ammonia.

"Miss Alice?" I hear a voice.

The woman who snaps me back into reality is short and

plump, clothed head to toe in a happy blue print. I recognize her instantly—Nurse Sadie—she's the same woman who told me about my sister's cancer. Her hands are tar black, bearing long fake nails painted red with tiny, diamond-like studs.

"These are for you," she tells me.

I hear the words and try to move my head, but I can't. I see a bundle of folded papers wrapped tightly in a red rubber band.

"Miss Alice?" the woman says again, stooping a little closer. "You might want to take a look. She left this for you."

At these words—*she left*—synapses begin to fire again. *She left? No. She can't possibly have left. Not again. Not like this. Look, she's right there.*

Sadie sets the papers on my lap, sliding them under my fingers, which have now fallen lifeless. I feel the cool, smooth texture and instinctively clamp down like my life depends on it—like the only thing keeping me from flying into oblivion are these papers I hold so dear.

It takes great effort, but my head finally moves. I look up into her dark features, her kind yet distant face. She doesn't look like I might have expected a bearer of bad news to look. Her black hair is in big curls around her head, and remnants of deep red lipstick line the edges of her full mouth.

A feeling wells up in me, fierce like a volcano bubbling. It's the first time I've felt anything in I don't know how long. All at once, I want to hug Sadie—and hit her as hard as I can. I do neither. Instead, I focus on that old adage:

Don't kill the messenger.

I cling to it—allowing me to feel nothing more. I get it now. *Ha.* It's almost funny. This woman is just the messenger. And anyway, killing her won't do any good. My baby sister is still lying there in front of me, not moving. And I have her papers to read now. And questions to be answered. How in the world could Honor have cancer and me not know a thing about it? And how could she be in town for so long without telling me? Something simply doesn't add up.

Honor

It feels strange, Alice. Writing, I mean. You know, I've always dreamed of being a writer or artist, someone creative, sitting on the sands of Nantucket in an oversized beach hat and movie star sunglasses. And you're sitting right next to me, sipping sangria and reveling in the sunshine. You don't let me take my life too seriously. That's what I love about you. Please know how much I love you.

When I wrote those little Nancy Drew-type mysteries in the early nineties, I remember plucking away at my typewriter while Jack was at work. He never knew about my closet life. I would never have dreamed of letting him in, what with his starched white shirts and numbers that always added up. But you read them. You've always been my reader, my cheerleader, keeping your snickers to yourself. You're my biggest fan. And I am yours.

So I suppose this is all fitting. I'm going to let you be my reader one more time. You're the one person in the world who will actually understand.

This being the closest thing I have to a last will and testament, I'm stumped. I have nothing really to leave behind. I never had children, never did any great deeds. I have no money to my name, no legacy, truly, to think of. But I want you to understand what's happened. You deserve at least that much.

Alice

I pull Honor's letter to my chest, and the weight of it pins me down. I can't go on. Not now. I close my eyes and wonder if they'll ever open. And I wait to keep reading until my heart starts beating again.

Clearwater, Florida
March 3, 2006

Honor

To begin with, I know you never understood why I "lived in sin" with Brett for so long. Not that you ever judged me. You didn't. There were a million reasons why I wouldn't marry him, not the least being that I'd done it before with Jack. Marriage was certainly no trophy in my case.

Brett and I had a strange sort of relationship. Have you ever had a pair of panties that look atrocious and don't fit your rear anymore, yet you keep them in the drawer for some reason? Why? For proof that you fit into them once? For me it was more like a daily reminder that I didn't deserve better than holey underwear.

Our relationship had deteriorated like moths to cotton. I'd given him everything I had in me—my youth, my enthusiasm. He, in return, had given me plenty—a hard time, bad credit, even lower self-esteem, a sexually transmitted disease. Sorry, I know that's shocking, but it is one reason why I stayed with him for so long. I was corroded and unworthy of anyone else. You don't know how difficult it is to say this to you, Alice, but you, especially, need to hear this.

I remember just before I left Brett, I was sitting on the couch in our Florida bungalow reading a self-help book when he barged into the house, hungry for lunch. I'd stopped what I was doing to make him a diet shake—he was always dieting and hated the way he looked. And I shouldn't have done it, but I opened up.

"I'm reading this book about discovering your inner self," I told him. "You know, like uncovering your subconscious mind, discovering the unknown. Anyway, I'm having a problem."

"What is it?" he asked, slurping his milkshake and staring into the mirror at his growing physique.

"You're supposed to describe yourself in ten words or less,

and I can't do it. I've been sitting here all morning and I've only come up with three pitiful words."

Brett thought a minute and then turned to me. There was a long moment of silence when we just stared at each other. All I could hear was the sound of the fan, churning our stagnant air.

Then he said, "Got it. Beautiful and ugly."

"What?"

"That's two more words to describe you," he said. "You are absolutely the most beautiful *ugly* woman in the world. When you get dressed up, you're as hot as they come. But boy, you sure can do ugly. It's like you're two different people."

"I beg your pardon," I snipped. "I am not ugly."

"Honor, baby, you've got ugly down pat. The clothes you wear—*ugly*—baggy things that never match. And your hair, well, just look at it! And then there's the no makeup." He walked over to me and put his fingers on my cheek. He seemed to be studying my gray hairs, my oversized pores, my acne scars. "Put on some makeup, would you, babe?"

Then he charged out of the room and took all the air with him. He had turned the fan off, and I began to suffocate. I ran to the windows and opened all of them until a warm breeze filled my lungs.

I finally sat back down with my book and worked for a good hour or so. I was driving myself crazy. Every few minutes I'd get up to go look at myself in the mirror. *Ugly? He really thinks I'm ugly?* I was always so beautiful. That's what people told me.

Anyway, you called and broke my focus like an angel. Do you remember this?

"Honor, hey, it's Alice."

"Hey, how's everything? Everybody all right?"

"Yes," you told me in your sweet voice. "I just wanted to see what you're doing."

I knew what you were calling about, though. I'd let you down—again. We had started a family business together, cakes and cookies. We'd dreamed of becoming the next two Mrs. Fields, and I was gung-ho in the beginning, but then I left. I did that to you. And you were up to your ears in cookies. You needed me. I wasn't there.

"I'm reading one of those in-depth psychological books and not having an easy go of it," I told you, not that you'd ever be caught dead reading a book like that. "I'm beginning to think I have noodles for brains. Did Mother drop me on my head as a baby?"

"Don't be ridiculous," you said. "It's from getting whacked with a baseball bat. You remember that? You were ten I think."

"You could be right because listen to this. I can only come up with three words to describe myself—retired, young, and broke."

"You're not retired, Honor. You're just not working."

"Same thing. Anyway, I did much better on the next exercise. You're supposed to write down ten words that do *not* describe you—adjectives you would deny ever being."

"That's easy," you told me, "just one word—married."

"Ha ha. Not the adjective I had in mind. I wrote: Arrogant. Impatient. Selfish. Untrustworthy. Unorganized. Rude. Grumpy. Liar. Uncaring. Stupid. Then I read further in the book—the words to *not* describe you are actually who you are!"

"Calm down, Honor. That doesn't mean you're a bad person."

"Doesn't it though? Well then it said to write an argument supporting each word, and it was easy! Stupid: because of previous mistakes resulting in an unsettled life with only five dollars to my name. Uncaring: I haven't seen my family much in the past five years. Liar: people think I'm ultra-successful. Grumpy: because I haven't succeeded. I couldn't write anymore, Alice. This is all true! All of it!"

"Calm down, Honor."

"I can't calm down! Then it said to draw a picture of myself and I did. It's the closest to self-analysis I've ever gotten. It looks just like me!"

"Send me the picture and I'll let you know what I think."

"All right. You know, Alice, maybe I'm not ready to find myself just yet. What if I find myself, and I really don't like me?"

"You've got to stop reading those books," you told me, filled as usual with practicality. "I love you just the way you are." And I know you meant it. You just didn't know how much of me I was holding back from you.

I never sent you that picture I drew, Alice. Sorry. I said I was a liar and untrustworthy, remember? Instead I held on to it and studied it—how ugly it was—the huge eyes and flimsy lines, the overbearing scowl. It would serve as a launching pad for my new career as an artist. It was the first of my self-portrait series.

Just five months later, I would paint my last.

11

St. Anne's Isle
July 23, 2006

Honor

I could see from my window the sun high over the ocean, glittering off waves rolling in. It was almost noon. After several days of playing hooky from my playground nanny lessons and suffering alone in my room, I finally received the dreaded knock at my door. I'd been expecting it. I'd wondered why Duchess hadn't harped on me to go—she'd pretty much left me alone. So I was ready for her, I suppose. I simply was not ready for who I saw when I turned the knob.

"Oh, sorry for botherin' you, ma'am. You Honor Maddox?"

The man at the door had a close-crop of blonde curly hair and suntanned forearms. His eyes were dark and intense, set beneath a heavy brow. I would have thought he was handsome had I not been thoroughly terrified by what he was wearing. On the chest pocket of his starched blue shirt was a brass badge. Of all the nerve, Duchess had called the police!

My mind swam and sank at the same time, trying to think of ways to escape. I could dart for the sliding glass door and jump over the balcony. It probably wouldn't do the job though. I'd be maimed with a broken leg or hip, and he'd still take me away to the loony bin. I struggled to remain composed but eventually mustered some Southern charm and said, "Yes, that's me. Can I help you, officer?"

He seemed to be staring, not at me, but at the room behind me. Was he looking for a weapon? Did he think I was dangerous? I'd never felt so tried and convicted in all my life! I'd been caught red-handed, contemplating suicide! I'd been doing it the second he'd knocked. And he knew it. I could tell.

Duchess

Mr. Cutie Pie Officer said in a deep, official voice, "Uh, ma'am, Miss Anne here was worried about you. Said she hasn't seen you in a couple days." I knew that was the first time Honor'd heard my real name. I slid out from behind him and showed my face, wearing a very sane and civilized pant suit. I was grinning like the white-haired devil I am and pointing to his rear end. I fanned my cheeks and put the back of my hand up to my forehead like all of a sudden it was real hot in there next to Mr. Hot Pants With A Gun.

Honor was floored I'd called in the law, and she tried to think real quick. "I'm so sorry for causing concern. I just haven't been feeling well." Then turning to me she said, "My goodness! You didn't have to call the police. You could have just come up and checked on me yourself, you old silly." She glared at me, a look enough to fry my behind.

"Yes, but then you'd never have met the strappin' Officer Simmons, now would you?" The officer turned bright red and cleared his throat.

"Uh, well, if you ladies are all right, I'll just be goin' then," he said, turning to face me. "Nice to see you again, Miss Anne."

"You too, sweetie. Hope I didn't cause you any trouble now. How's your mama doin' these days?"

"Doin' real good. Thanks for askin'. She's gettin' 'round pretty well ever since her hip got fixed."

"Oh that's nice. Such a sweet lady. She been workin' in that pretty garden of hers?"

"A little, yes ma'am. I've been tryin' to help her out with her mowin' and such. You know how it is."

"You're such a good boy. Tell your mama I said 'hey' now, hear?"

"I'll do that," he said, backing away.

"Oh, Officer Simmons," I said, making him stop, "Miss Honor here looks a little peaked, don't you think? Would you mind escortin' her to the playground? She's meetin' Miss Blondell there in just a bit. Aren't you, Honor? Blondell's become quite fond of her, you know."

The officer turned to Honor and she went all self-conscious. Had no makeup on and her hair was slicked back, still wet from taking a shower. At least she was clean.

"I reckon I could do that. I'm goin' right past there. You 'bout ready, ma'am?"

"Oh please, don't ma'am her, son," I scolded, "and don't ma'am me, neither. There's nothing to make a woman feel older than bein' ma'amed half to death. Her name is Honor."

He looked like he might die a thousand deaths. "Sorry, m— Miss Honor. You 'bout ready then?"

"Oh no," she said, grabbing her throat. "I really don't think so."

"But she's waitin' for you, Honor." I turned the knife in her chest. "You can't leave an old woman waitin' on you. Go on." I winked.

"Well, okay, but I can go on my own. I've got to dry my hair and all. It'll be awhile. You just go on," she told him. "Thank you though."

"Oh, I can wait," he said real innocent. I just love that boy. "I'm not due back at the station for another hour. I don't mind. Really. I got nothin' better to do."

"You see that, Honor? Officer Simmons here doesn't mind waitin' for you."

The air was thick with tension and there was Honor—stuck in the strangest place. But sport that she was, she decided to play along. At least she was being pulled out of her despair by a fine-looking man this time. Shucks, you'd have to *pay* me not to go with that man.

"Give me just a few minutes then," she told him.

Honor

I shut the door and leaned up against it, actually smiling. I was surprised at how exhilarated I felt, running around the room, trying to find something decent to wear. I had no makeup to put on, no way to hide the bags that seemed to be multiplying under my eyes, but I tousled my hair dry and hoped for the best. I told myself at least I wasn't being hauled off in handcuffs. And as Officer Simmons and I walked out the front door, his fingers grazing the small of my back, I made a mental note not to underestimate the Duchess anymore.

Duchess

"If you run into Sonny, say 'hey' to him for me, hear?" I said before the door shut. "Tell him don't be such a stranger. I promise I don't bite." I winked, and off they went.

I knew full well what I was doing when I called Officer Simmons over to the house that day. Now there's a man. Through and through. Not only does he have dark, sexy eyes to light a fire in your bosom, but he's kind as they come and loves his mama. Not that he's a mama's boy, because he's not. I can't stand that—when a man can't do a thing for you without asking his mama what she needs done first.

Mackey was like that. Always a mama's boy. Not that she was even living when we married. She'd died just two years before I met him, but the ghost of that old woman was so real, we kept a room for her in the back of the house. It's where she'd always lived, and I wasn't allowed to touch it when I moved in. I figured that's just how people did things, you know. I didn't know better.

Mercy on my soul, I could not live up to that dead woman's expectations. "Can't you make meatloaf like my mama?" Mackey would say. "She put ketchup on the top." Or, "Annie, how many times have I told you, you have to iron the creases *into* my pants like this. Not out! My mama would have had this whole pile done and hung by now—*plus* supper on the table!"

I couldn't stand Mackey's mama, no harm intended. I never met the woman, but she ruled me from the day I moved in.

Anyway, back to Honor and Officer Simmons. I figured, if this handsome man can't bring Honor out of her black dismal turtle shell, I did not know what could. Who knows, something might could happen between them. It could. Honor still had her looks, and Officer Simmons was still single, hallelujah. You could search the whole world over and not find a better man. If I'd had a daughter I would have picked him out for her, just the same. *Nothin' gained without tryin',* as Mama used to say.

12

Honor

I tried hard to ignore the sound of the officer breathing next to me as we walked down the road. Roots buckled through the asphalt, and as the road became bumpier, I knew we were getting close to the playground. There was something sensual about our walking together—about him. I hated that. I'd always been attracted to the wrong kind of men, yet here I was, finding myself oddly aroused by this one. It was surely the kiss of death for him. It could only mean he was trouble—something I wanted no part of.

Instead I paid close attention to the feel of the warm breeze blowing through my hair, as if I'd just realized I had hair. I felt the smooth caress of the wind on my arms. My senses had awakened after days—or years—of slumber.

I'm fairly sure Officer Simmons was talking to me while his feet kept pace with mine, but I can't tell you anything he said, and I can't say I ever replied to him. Finally, as we approached the palmetto-flanked entry to the park, my ears opened to hear children's voices and suddenly, I heard a man's.

"... said you been pretty upset, so I don't take any offense. My mama always told me, 'Boy, if you could just open your ears half as much as you flap your lips, you might just make it in this world.' Miss Blondell's a lot like my mama. Oh, there she is now. Hey there, Miss Blondell! How you been?"

I stared at the beautiful (okay, now he was looking beautiful) man beside me as he left my side and went to Blondell. He bent down and hugged her hard and motioned my way. Blondell grinned up at him and then looked over at me as I shuffled through playground mulch. She had a funny look on her face like she'd just heard a good joke. I was imagining I was the butt of it. I tried to shake it off and acted like I'd simply run into this fine officer on my way there.

"So nice to see you, Blondell. Look who I ran into. You two must be old friends."

"Oh, we go way back," said the officer, grinning at Blondell and squeezing her around her shoulders. He left her and walked around the circle of nannies, grabbing hands and chit-chatting away.

"So that's St. Anne's police department," I said to Blondell, smiling despite myself.

"E' good bo', sho'nuff. Good ya come, On'ry."

Blondell said my name like Daddy used to tease. He'd call me "Ornery" instead of "Honor" in his Southern twang. And it fit. I'd always been ornery, still to that day.

"Sit down ya," she said.

When I sat on an overturned palmetto trunk, the nannies followed, and things settled down. They said their hellos to me, and Officer Simmons said his goodbyes. He glanced at me before he left and nodded. "Bye now," he said.

My hand lifted to a wave and my lips were pursed to say the same, but he had already turned. He walked away much quicker than he'd come.

"You feelin' okay, Miss Honor?" squeaked Ruby. "We been missin' you."

"Thanks, Ruby. I'm feeling better. Must've been coming down with something." That's the excuse I gave her. Blondell didn't buy it.

"Gettin' long wid Duchess?" she asked me.

"Oh yes," I sang. "Just fine. Just fine."

"Mm hmm. T'ought you migh'." She said, trying to hide a grin.

I attempted to read Blondell as she was surely doing me. She was far wiser than I'd realized. She'd paired me with the

Duchess—a kindred spirit. The more I found to dislike about Duchess, the more I realized we were one and the same.

"She's quite a character," I said, filling empty space.

"Duchess? She ain mean nuttin' bad," said Blondell, quickly coming to her rescue. "Heart don' mean eb'ryt'ing de mout' say."

"Yes sir, she's harmless," said Willa, scooting closer to me on the tree trunk. "That woman's been through a lot now. Lord have mercy. I can 'member Duchess back when she was all messed up. 'Member that?"

"Oh, I remember," said Ruby. "Miss Honor, you think you in a bad way these days? You ain't seen nothin' till you seen the Duchess few years back. Barely knew her own name or nothin'. If it weren't for Miss Blondell taking her in, we'd be visiting Duchess over to the graveyard."

"Ain dat righ'," said Blondell, staring at the soil and rocking back and forth.

"You mean when she lost her children?" I asked, trying to fit into the conversation.

"Her chill'ren?" Ruby clucked her tongue. "Girl, I'm talking 'bout her dog."

"Good Lawd, that dawg!" The nannies started laughing and slapping knees.

Then Willa's big arm nudged me and she whispered, "No really, Miss Honor. She's a fine lady. Try to see the good in Duchess if you can. We all need that, don't we? Somebody to see the good?"

"Yes we do," I told her. Yes we do.

As I was walking back to the mansion past white gardenias in withering bloom, it came to me then, some worthless piece of drivel I'd read in a self-help book once. But perhaps it was true. If I learned to accept the things I couldn't stand about Duchess, was it possible I might be able to tolerate my own sad self?

I wondered if this had all been orchestrated by Blondell. I envisioned her as this puppet master pulling my strings and making me dance, but then I thought, *No. She's just an old lady. I'm the one growing. I'm the one learning to solve my own issues. I don't need Gullah nannies telling me how to fix my life.* Quite proud of myself as I moved up the driveway and mounted the steps, I devised a little self-help experiment: I would stop focusing on me and my problems for a change—and instead, I would try to find ways to help the Duchess have a fulfilling existence. I could do it. I was creative. And for this, I would *have* to get creative. Duchess was quite an unusual piece of work.

13

Waccamaw Memorial Hospital,
Murrells Inlet
December 11, 2006

Alice

"I'm at the hospital," I tell my husband, Wayne. He inhales sharply on the other end of the phone line.

"The hospital! What happened? Are you all right? Dangit, I've been worried sick, wondering where you were!"

I can picture the vein in his right temple bulging. "I'm fine," I say. "I broke some toes. I wrecked the car."

"You wrecked—oh my—Alice, are you sure you're all right?"

"I'm fine."

I hold the phone away from my ear as Wayne spews expletives

like a geyser. "I knew this would happen! I told you not to drive in this mess. Didn't I, honey? Didn't I? What in the world is wrong with you, Alice? Why don't you ever listen to me?"

I don't respond.

After a pause he says, "I'll be right there. Don't move."

"No, don't," I say. "I'm staying here."

"You're what? Is it that bad? Don't tell me you're—"

"No, I'm fine, but—" Tears well up. "Honor's here," I whisper.

"Honor? What do you mean? I thought you said she wasn't coming till Friday."

"She wasn't."

"Then what in the world is going on? Why is *she* there with you?" He's jealous, and at this moment, I'm wishing it *was* him there in front of me unconscious instead of her.

"She's sick!" I scream and then start sobbing.

Wayne stays quiet on his end. Finally he says, "What's wrong with her?"

"She has cancer, Wayne. She's not doing well at all."

"I'm coming to get you, Alice."

"No! You're not."

"What do you mean, *no*? Sarah and Melody are coming home tomorrow, Alice! Now cut this out and come on home. I'm sorry about Honor, but she's in the hospital, right? That's what it's there for—sick people."

"Are you kidding me?"

Pause. "I didn't mean it that way. I'm sorry, honey, I just—"

"There's leftover pot roast in the fridge. Heat it up. I'm staying here with Honor tonight."

Click.

I turn my cell phone off. I've never hung up on him before, and I've never stayed away from Wayne. I don't think he can handle it. Could never work the microwave. Heaven help him if he actually has to make his own coffee in the morning. I don't care. With his temper, I half expect him to storm the hospital at some point tonight. He hasn't always been that way though—at least that's what he likes to tell me. When he loses control, Wayne says it's because I bring out the worst in him.

Like *I* do it. I *force* him to act that way.

Honor can't stand him. You know it's bad when your own sister refuses to call him by name. She refers to him as "what's-his-face" or "Mr. Man," implying I live in *Misery*. Like the movie. I hate it when she does that. My life with Wayne isn't great, but it is what it is.

I watch a new nurse come in and check Honor's vital signs. She scribbles something in her chart. "Dr. So-and-so is on his way in. He'll speak with you when he gets here, okay?"

I nod absentmindedly. He isn't named "So-and-so" but he might as well be. A great fog has taken over me. My eyes are swollen from crying. I'm somewhere outside my body, watching Honor. *Where is she? Is she just asleep? Is she in a coma? Will she wake up?* I scoot up next to her and grab her hand. The window is behind me. Someone has come in and shut the curtains. It's dark outside and the clock says 10:50. I can hear it ticking, pressing for the next minute and the next and the next.

I pull out Honor's memoir and carefully straighten it. I study her handwriting. It's beautiful, just like she is—always the same loopy loops and happy *Ms*. More tears form, and I press them away with my shirt sleeve. I need to read some more. I'm in the dark about so much.

Honor

I was beautiful once. There was a point in my life when I knew I was beautiful—back when my hair was long and silky and my green eyes innocent. When I went to St. Anne's I could hardly look at them. I felt nauseated simply looking into my own eyes. Can you imagine? All I saw then was ugliness.

He'd called me ugly. He'd said my pants were too baggy and my face was hideous without makeup. Brett, with his bulging beer belly and multiplying chins.

I'd gone to St. Anne's Isle to get away from it all—from him, from Florida, from me. I thought the ocean would be healing—that the water would wash over me, leaving my misery to evaporate like dew in the sunshine. It didn't work. Nothing worked.

I had left the only man in my life, and I was unemployed. I

liked to call it retirement, even though officially, I was still ten years away from retirement age. And I know you said I could stay with you, but I had to get away. I needed a place far enough away that I could reinvent myself—completely.

When I turned onto Highway 17 North in South Carolina I was playing roulette—I had no idea where to go, where I should start over. But when I saw the sign for St. Anne's Isle, I nearly put my Jetta in a tailspin to make the turn. I don't know what made me do it—it just felt right.

St. Anne's was close enough to Murrells Inlet that I could be there in a heartbeat if you really needed me, but it was far enough away for me to forge my own life. And I'd thought to myself, *Positive thinking, visualization, that's all you need.* I'd read all the books, trust me. I figured if I could just surround myself with those people I wanted to be—those rich, fabulous people with the shiny Jaguars and pants that always fit just right—if I could be around them and their happy little families, children even, then it might happen for me. There was a chance it would happen for me.

I was wrong. Oh, how wrong I was.

Nothing good happened for me. Ever. And do you know why? Because I didn't deserve it. There are laws in the universe. Justice exists, you know. God is vengeful. And He'd given me my just deserts. It was all right though. I was okay with that. I was really okay. I thought so anyway until I tried to kill myself.

Alice

I close the paper, crumpling it. I don't think I can do this. I can't possibly go on. *I have failed her so badly! I'm not there for her enough. I wasn't there when she needed me! What kind of a sister am I?*

It takes a few minutes of me cursing myself before I can go on. But I do. I have to.

Honor took sleeping pills. She *wanted* to die? I just can't believe it—not her. But the words on the paper don't lie. I'm seeing a whole new side to Honor I never knew existed.

She was saved by some black women who took her in. She went to live with a naked woman called "the Duchess."

Black nannies? Naked ladies? Honor wanted to die?

I think I just might be losing my mind.

I place the papers on my leg and lean my head back. I feel like I'm reading a novel. This is someone else's life. But it sounds so much like Honor, I know it's real.

I remember years ago when she was living in Houston, just after she married Jack. She would write detective stories and send them to me to read, and I loved them. I'm a voracious reader, and I'd put her stories right up there with the bestsellers. She was as good as any of them, and should have been published but never was. There was always something holding Honor back from fulfilling her dreams. For that matter, there was something holding me back too.

Murrells Inlet

February 2000

Honor

When what's-his-face left us alone, we had some good times together. Didn't we, Alice? We were always so resourceful—such entrepreneurs. I usually had all the cockamamie ideas and you were the one to follow through long after I'd lost interest and petered out.

But there was always *something*. We'd find a new craft, the project du jour, and we were always so certain we'd wind up millionaires, never having to depend on a man again for the rest of our lives. Or was that just me who felt that way? No, I'm pretty sure you were dying to have your own nest egg hidden away for the day when you might decide to leave you-know-who. None of my business, I know, but . . . oh well. I'm not one for keeping my mouth shut, now am I?

Remember when we were going to "make it big" selling decoupage plates and boxes and knickknacks? We had gone to the library to do some research on how two women with no money could make an absolute fortune. We'd already done homemade lollipops. That was a bust. Too much work for too little money. So there we were in that hushed little place when I found an article about a lady out west who'd cut out pictures from wrapping paper and glued them onto flower vases and furniture. How hard could that be? She was an overnight success with people clamoring to buy her "artwork." I was so excited I wanted to scream! I was positive you and I would make a gazillion dollars *and* be famous to boot.

But then, ahem, *you* had forgotten your library card and we couldn't check anything out. Not saying that it was your fault, but . . .

I *swear* I had never shoplifted before. But we *needed* that article. It was our ticket to freedom. So I stuck the little magazine under my shirt. It was nothing, really. Probably cost the library a dollar to replace. Gee wiz. But the buzzer went off when we tried to leave, remember? *The buzzer went off!*

Have you ever been so mortified? I'll never forget the look on your face when that squirrelly woman was waggling her finger in front of our noses. You couldn't show your face in the library for a long time after that. And you never even scolded me for it. You were just quiet on the drive home and didn't even mention it again.

You've always been like that—protecting my dignity. I love you for that, Alice. And I'm so sorry for leaving, really I am, but I didn't have to see any of those people again—you, on the other hand, no such luck. See what hanging around with your little sister gets you? Trouble, trouble, *trouble.* I think in some way I figured you'd be better off without me if I left. I know it's a lame excuse. I can't apologize enough.

Well, our decoupage days were limited, although fun. You were much better at it than I was. You had tons more patience and never got those irritating lumps of air underneath your pictures. My work always turned out lumpy and shifty—just like me. Ha. Like me.

That was a long time ago. It almost seems like another lifetime, doesn't it?

Alice

My painkillers are wearing off. My foot is burning, propped up on Honor's bed. She still hasn't moved.

I hear a soft knock at the door. A woman wheels in a blood pressure machine and sticks a cuff on Honor's arm. She pumps it up and slowly lets the air out. We don't speak. Then the door swings open and a doctor walks in.

"How's she doing?" he asks.

"I don't know. You tell me." I'm irreverent, very unlike me, but I don't care. I realize he was addressing the nurse instead and I shuffle my papers, wrapping them back in the rubber band. The doctor looks over Honor's chart and then pulls up a chair next to me.

"Is there nothing we can do for her?" I ask, helpless.

"We've tried. I am sorry."

"But there has to be something! We can't just let her get worse!"

"Miss—I know this is hard to digest, but your sister is—well, she's shutting down now."

"Shutting down? You mean she's dying." Saying those words sends a new wave of panic through me and I become painfully alert. "How long? When?" I ask.

"Anytime, really. Soon," he says.

"Soon." I look at Honor, dying there in front of me, and wish I could switch places with her. The instant I do, I'm flooded with terror and guilt. My girls are coming home tomorrow.

"But I don't understand," I plead. "How did this happen?"

"Your sister was brought here a few weeks ago. She had collapsed at a gas station in Litchfield."

"A gas station?" My eyes dart back and forth as I try to focus and make sense of it all.

"We were surprised she was doing as well as she was—that she'd made it this long with no treatment."

"No treatment?" I am aware I'm repeating everything back to him in question form, but I can't do anything to change it.

"I know it's difficult to understand," he says, "but apparently, your sister had known she was sick for some time. For whatever reason, she opted not to treat her cancer. Until she came here, that is. She's been quite urgent to find a miracle. We tried radiation to relieve a large tumor on her brain. But there's really nothing else we can do now. She's inoperable. I'll have someone from hospice come in and speak with you in the morning. But for now, you might want to read over this."

He hands me a pink pamphlet. I peer down at the title: *Saying Goodbye.* I look back up at him and he tells me again,

"I'm very sorry. We'd like to make you as comfortable as you can be while you're here. I'll have a cot brought in."

"Thank you," I say, though I have no idea what in the world I'm thanking him for.

14

Honor

On St. Anne's Isle, my latest scheme was to help myself through helping someone else. Duchess needed *tons* of help. She was extremely busy doing positively nothing. She would spend her days spinning her wheels, walking around the house, naked mostly, with a fretted look on her face. She reminded me so much of the White Rabbit in *Alice in Wonderland*. I loved that book. She'd act as if she'd forgotten something in the other room, spouting out, "Oh no, what am I forgetting . . ." every now and then.

But I never saw her do one blasted thing. And filth was all around her, except for the kitchen, of course. When Duchess would sit down on the fur-covered furniture with her bare rear-end, I thought I'd lose my mind.

Duchess

"Did you have a pet?" Honor asked me, finally. I was dreading the day. I stared at her with a whatever-makes-you-think-that look on my face.

"It's just . . . there's hair everywhere. I thought you might have had a dog or something."

"Aaaaaaaaawwww, Fluffy!" Shucks, I went off like a grenade. "Fluffy! Oh my baby, I miss herrrr! Fluffy, Fluffy, my sweet little Fluffy!" My heart ripped to shreds again, and I buried my head in my hands and boo-hoo'd. I didn't think I'd ever be able to stop.

I was naked, so Honor consoled me as best a body can do from clear 'cross the room. Didn't want to touch me, I reckon. "You poor thing," she said. "I'm so sorry."

I waved her off and ran on out the back door. I needed to see the great big ocean and know there's a whole world of folks hurtin' just like me. I think that every time I look out to the water. Each ripple to me is a sliver of somebody's sorrow, just a-washing away.

I stuck a frisky hermit crab on my mound of shells in memory of sweet Fluffy, and don't you know that booger just walked away with better things to do. I figured it was time to pull myself together then. I climbed the steps and walked through the house, calling, "Honor? Yoo hoo. Everything's all right now. Don't worry, dear. I'm all right."

And boy, you should have seen my face when I realized what Honor was up to.

"What you doin'?" I asked her, my jaw dropped. She was kneeling down, scrubbing the hardwoods in my foyer.

"Cleaning," she beamed. "Someone's got to," she mumbled under her breath. I heard her though. Stinker. I was thinking hard then, trying to remember exactly what I'd said to get her to do such a thing, cleaning like that. My eyes, I know, practically crossed, and normally I suck in my bare flabby stomach, but at this moment, boy howdy, I let it all hang out. And let me tell you, it was bigger than I'd given it credit for.

"Just for the record," Honor told me, clearing her throat, "I hate cleaning. Hate it. Capital 'H' hate. But you need this. Heck, I need this too," she murmured, picking up the corner of a rug and checking the dirt underneath. Well now, I wasn't about to argue with her. The girl had her mind set to clean, so have at it. Heaven knows I needed a fresh start myself. Having the hair of a loved one spread out everywhere makes it near impossible to stop grieving—and having a body actually care and offer me help was like a cool breeze in hundred-degree weather. Unexpected and refreshing.

I did so enjoy my new clean kitchen, and I looked at Honor

there on her knees and thought, *That sneaky Blondell—knew just what I needed, sending this child my way.*

When I realized I was still naked, I skittered off, flab flying every which way, and when I came back, I was wearing a pair of sweatpants and a T-shirt. Ready to work! I'd pulled my hair back best as I could in a tiny white ponytail, and I had my latex gloves on and a white painter's mask over my face.

Honor didn't say a word to me but scrubbed and scrubbed, dipping her hand in a bucket of water and making the floor shine. Like Cinderella she was. I watched her, my head going back and forth, back and forth with the movement of her hand. Then I ran off again to get my old avocado green vacuum cleaner. I was so excited. I spun the cord around and around and ran to the wall to plug it in. I was smiling so big—and for cleaning, no doubt! What a miracle. Honor was smiling too, her eyes crinkled up to near invisible.

We cleaned for a full day: the rugs, the furniture, the floors, the walls, the windows. Room after room after room. I even put some music on. Beach music and R&B filled the house like a happy choir. We hummed and we sang, we danced and even shagged with each other. We were in full mania—high as two seagulls soaring toward the sun.

By the end of the day, I was exhausted—and elated—something I hadn't felt in a long, long time. I could barely move and hobbled when I walked.

"This calls for a celebration, my dear," I said, picking up the telephone and spinning the dial. "Hello, Carlos? How are you, sweetie? This is Miss Anne on Sandy Point. Yes, I'm doin' just fine! Super! Listen, I'd just love for you to bring us two of your scrumptious seafood platters with all the trimmin's and lots of tartar sauce. What's that? Why, fried, of course! Can you do that for me, love? Oh, that'd be wonderful. Just put that on my bill now, hear? See you soon, sweetie pie. Bye-bye now."

Anne. I'd said my name again. Honor stared at me, and I could see she'd made the connection now. Anne. Like the island.

Soon as I hung up the receiver I said, "I came back to this island because of the name, you know. As a child I thought they'd named the island after me. Isn't that funny? Hmmph. Children, the things they can think." I laughed a little. "Saint Anne. Ha! Yep, that's me." I sat down on the sofa and rubbed my hand over the freshly cleaned fabric. Honor sat by me and did the same. I watched her hand slow to a stop, and she closed her eyes, settling into the cushions and resting her head on the back.

In two minutes flat, Honor was snoring long and loud, surprising for such a little thing. When the food arrived, I didn't have the heart to wake her—I'd never seen her so peaceful. So I stuck her meal in the fridge, poured myself a nice glass of crisp chardonnay, and moved out onto the balcony to eat in the warm night air.

The ocean sang to me as it rolled up to the house. *Whoosh-ah, whoosh-ah.* I sipped my wine. *Whoosh.* I dipped a crispy fried shrimp into cool, creamy tartar sauce and savored it on my tongue. *Whoosh-ah.* The stars were bright, and I realized I'd kept Honor too busy to think about suicide for a full twelve hours. *Whoosh, you done good, Anne, whoosh-ah,* the ocean whispered to me. Heck, maybe she'd never even think of doing such an awful thing again.

The night was still and magical. I thought about Honor, what all she'd been through, what all she was going through now. I thought about her sister Alice and her two girls. I dreamed of a nice happy reunion someday. Of Honor doing something wonderful so she could face them all again, head held high. And for the first time in a long, long time, I saw I had a part in something grander than me. There were things I could do to help this child. All of a sudden my future seemed very real, and miracle of miracles, this old fool had hope.

I woke Honor up just before I went to bed and watched her eat every last thing on her plate. I was comforted by her healthy appetite. A woman who could eat like that, I knew, was a woman well on her way.

15

Alice

I wake up to the sound of wheels rolling. I open my eyes and don't know where I am. My head aches, my eyes are puffy, and my foot is throbbing. I realize I'm in a hospital and flash back to when I was giving birth to Sarah. I hated the hospital smell, hated the wallpaper, the sterile sounds, the strangers invading my privacy.

It takes me a minute to realize I'm not in the hospital for me. I'm here for Honor.

I jump up, startled by reality, and clutch at my heart. She

hasn't moved. She looks terrible. In the daylight, I can see her pallor is almost gray. And is it my imagination or are her cheeks caving in?

"Hey, Honor," I say, praying she can hear me. "I'm still here. I'm not leaving you. Ever. I'm going to be right here with you. Can you hear me, honey? I love you. I love you so much."

She doesn't respond.

I get up to use the bathroom on crutches. As I sit on the toilet, I wonder if Honor sat here a week ago. I just can't believe she's lying in there, unreachable, dying. I won't believe it. There has to be something we can do!

After I wash up, I hobble out into the hallway. I need to find a nurse but don't want to go too far away. Will she die today? I hurry back into the room at the thought and move to her side. I press the red nurse call button.

"Yes?"

"I need a nurse. I—can we get a nurse in here?"

"Someone will be right there."

The nurse who comes in is wearing pink scrubs. She's white with blonde hair in a ponytail. She looks to be about Honor's age. I wish this woman was lying in the bed instead of Honor, and instantly feel guilty for the thought.

"What do we do?" I ask her.

"What do you mean?"

"I mean . . . what do we do? What does she do? Do we just wait until she dies? How does she eat? Shouldn't someone be feeding her breakfast by now?"

"She . . . did you get a pamphlet on the stages of dying?"

"Yes, I did, but—"

"I just come in every few hours to take her vitals. I can ask the doctor to come speak with you when she comes in."

"She? I thought her doctor is a he."

"Yes, but Dr. Sherry is on this morning. I'll ask her to come speak with you. You might want to go down to the cafeteria and get some breakfast while she's on rounds."

"I'm not leaving her."

She appraises me and then says, "Oh, okay. I'll see if they can bring something up for you."

"Just coffee, please." I don't thank her. Very un-Southern. I move back to my chair by the window and stare at Honor, willing her to wake up.

I pick up the pink pamphlet on dying and start reading:

The final stages of life will bring about many physical and emotional changes. This can be a stressful time for both the dying person and loved ones. Although each terminal illness may present differently, some such as advanced cancer will show a steady decline toward death.

I pause when I hear another knock at the door. Expecting coffee from a cafeteria worker, my heart stops when I see my husband filling the door frame.

"Oh—*man*—" he says when he sees Honor lying there. I watch his face, watching her. There seems to be something there like pity, or maybe revulsion. I certainly don't see love in his eyes. "Man, oh man. What happened to her?"

I clutch my chest and turn to face the window. I can see pine trees blowing in the wind and blue skies peeking through. I want him to leave. I feel protective of Honor.

"Is she sleeping?" he asks. "Is she in a coma? What?"

"I don't know, Wayne. I don't know what's going on except— they say she's dying."

"Dying?" The silence between us solidifies.

"Oh man." Wayne rubs the back of his neck. "Well, the good thing is, she never had any kids."

"What?" I glare at him.

"I mean, it just wasn't meant to be, was it? With her—you know, this and all. It's just good there are no kids who are going to miss her."

"I will miss her, Wayne! She's my sister, for heaven's sake!"

"Look, babe. Don't freak out on me. I just came to get you home, all right? The girls are flying in soon, remember? We have to go to the airport."

I say nothing, but wrap my arms tighter around myself. Wayne walks around Honor's bed and picks up my crutches, trying them on for size. "If you'll notice, I haven't even said a word about you wrecking the car, have I? Come on, let's get outta here. She's not going anywhere."

I feel my teeth clench. "You need to pick up the girls yourself, Wayne. I'm staying. Right here."

"Dad-gummit, Alice!"

"Please, Wayne," I say through my teeth.

"Fine!" He leans the crutches back up against the wall and one falls down to the floor with a loud clatter. Both us of look over at Honor to see if she flinches.

She doesn't.

A skinny man in white knocks lightly on the door and pushes his way in, carrying a tray of food. Wayne turns and says, "How you doin'?" in his jovial, man's man sort of way. The guy smiles and sets the tray in front of me. I uncover the plastic cup of coffee and inhale. It smells like burned metal, but I'm so grateful for it.

"Don't tell the girls about Honor," I warn him. "Let me do that, please? Just bring them here, but call me on your way up, okay?"

"You got your cell phone? 'Cause I tried to call you a million times last night."

"I've got it," I tell him, not apologizing for refusing his calls. I pull out Honor's notes the second he leaves the room.

I must have dozed off. I was dreaming about the Duchess and Blondell and the nannies that Honor has described in detail. These people are becoming real to me—more real than the limp body lying in front of me or the endless strangers filing in and out of hospital room 221. I wish I could escape to St. Anne's Isle, anywhere but here.

But then again, I wouldn't dare be anywhere else.

I spot the *Saying Goodbye* brochure on the table next to Honor's letters. I hate the fact that they even had to make a pamphlet like this. It strikes me how many people must die in this hospital. In this very room perhaps.

The dying person may have peaks and valleys that falsely give the impression of recovery, I read.

I bow my head and pray to God. I tell Him He can break my other foot if I can see something, anything—some stirring or "peak" in Honor's condition—that might mean she's on her way to recovery. I'm staring at her, clutching her hand and waiting for my answer when my daughters walk in the door.

"Mom? Oh my gosh!" Sarah bursts into tears when she sees Honor lying there. Melody does the same and runs over to her bed.

"Aunt Honor? Mom, what's wrong?!" She's clearly terrified, hands covering her mouth.

"You were supposed to call me first!" I hiss at Wayne.

"They have a right to know," he says, as though he's concerned. He sits down in a chair near the door.

"Mom, what happened to you? What's going on?!"

So much for the glorious Norman Rockwell homecoming I've been practicing in my head for weeks. My girls are utterly destroyed, crying and terrified. Seeing them this way, though, allows me to take on the Mom role again, the one where I'm strong when they are weak. It's just what I need.

"Listen girls, come here." I pat a chair beside me and they both move to it, sitting together, limbs over limbs. Sarah puts her hand on my foot, but Melody can't take her eyes off Honor.

I take one hand from each of them and hold them tight. "Your Aunt Honor is very sick," I say. "She has cancer."

The girls suck in air. They don't move but look up at me for answers. "I just found out about this myself, so I know how big a shock it is."

"Is she going to be all right?" asks Melody. "Are they giving her chemo or anything?"

"They've tried." I grimace, feeling tears coming on. My nose runs, so I let go of their hands and grab a tissue from the box on the windowsill. I wish they didn't have to see me this way. Or see Honor this way.

"She's dying. Isn't she, Mom?" Sarah says with a scary maturity that seems beyond her years. All I can do is nod. My girls lean over and hug me tight. We shake silently with tiny gasps of air and tears falling between us.

Having them here with me, with Honor, feels good for a moment, but when I look into their eyes and see my daughters' despair, I realize two more people I love dearly are now stuck on this horrible sinking ship.

"Can you take them home?" I ask Wayne.

"No! We want to stay with you! We want to be here."

"I know you do, really, but I've got to talk to the doctors and I—I need to do this alone right now. I just need you both to go home and take care of your dad for me."

Translation: *Get him out of my hair.*

We all look over at Wayne. He gives us a little pathetic wave, assuring us he needs taking care of.

"See that? He needs you. Now, here's a list of groceries you can pick up."

"You sure, Mom? Please. We'd rather stay here with you . . ."

"No. Thank you, but no. I'm serious. I need someone in this family to have a normal holiday right now." The way I say it keeps them from fighting me anymore. They sniffle and walk to Honor's bed. They grab her hands and touch her legs through the blankets. Sarah leans over and kisses Honor's forehead, whispering to her. I can't hear what she's saying, but I can feel the weight of it.

Then they leave as I've asked, slumped over and defeated. As soon as the door closes I allow myself to cry again. I'm sitting in the bottom of a well, alone and with absolutely no way out.

16

St. Anne's Isle
July 30, 2006

Honor

When I woke up the next morning, the sun was streaming in across my feet in a band of gold. I filled my lungs and shoved my fingers under my pillow, feeling its coolness. I stuck my legs straight out for that perfect stretch you can only get at first light. I looked around the bedroom, mahogany wood oiled to a shine, windows clean enough to mistake for fresh air. Yes, I hated cleaning but just loved to reap the benefits later. I was reveling in my accomplishment. In those few moments, all seemed good with the world.

Until I remembered who I was.

I saw my clothes—the same ones I'd been wearing for days, borrowed clothes—piled in a heap on the floor beside the bed. My stomach rumbled. I remembered the seafood feast I'd had before bed, the deviled crab, the grouper fingers, and hushpuppies, light as air. My mouth watered and a terrible realization came over me. *We had no more food in the house.* One of us would have to go to the store. Of course, I should offer to go but—

I had no money.

Suddenly, the room began to close in on me. The walls, the floor, the ceiling with its fancy chandelier—all of it was fake. None of it was mine. What was I doing? Pretending to live here? Pretending this belonged to me? I wasn't really trying to help the Duchess, was I? I cleaned the house so I could take ownership of it in some small way. Didn't I? *Didn't I?* I bolted to my feet, panting and throwing the covers off my chest as if they were the culprit—as if the mere fabric was what kept me tied down in my place.

Crazed and queasy I ran to the little bath just in time to bring back what was left of dinner. I caught a glimpse of myself in the mirror and remembered my dancing and singing the night before, my futile acts of pretending to be happy. Lines creased my face where a smile should go. Wrinkles. Age. Futility. Trapped.

I rushed to the door, the one that was boarded up, and began pulling with all my strength on the wood. I jerked and pried and the nails began to give. One by one, I brought the boards down with superhuman strength. My fingers were raw and bleeding by the time the cool air from the house flooded over me. I breathed in scents of orange and lemon clean until I thought my lungs would pop. Then my veins seemed to deflate, and everything was all wrong, all black, all spinning.

Duchess

I got there as fast as I could. I was standing over her, breasts sagging near her face. I hated being naked then, but I'd no time to dress when I heard the ruckus. I held a wet cloth on her forehead saying, "There, there, now. You all right?" I kept feeling for a pulse, and when Honor opened her eyes, she looked away. I covered my bosoms in shame.

"Sweetie? You all right now? You gave me quite a scare," I said, studying her. "Do you think you can get up? Let's get you back in the bed. We got to get some food in you!"

I hauled her to her feet, holding her sides, and pulled Honor through the new doorway. "Now let's go back in here. My goodness, did you do this by yourself? Well, of course you did, but my goodness . . ." I sat her at the edge of the bed, and she stayed quiet. She was green. Honor crawled down under the covers and put her head down.

"You just get some rest now. I'm goin' to run to the store and stock up on some groceries. I've been meanin' to do that—well, the kitchen is clean now, you know. You and me, we're gonna eat right today! First though, you rest, Honor sweet thing you. I'll bring you somethin' just lickety-split."

I pressed her arm, but her eyes were already closed. She could probably hear me tiptoeing around the mess of boards and nails. I looked back at Honor in awe of her strength. She'd forced open a door I'd nailed shut years ago. And now here I was, walking right through like it never even existed. That was a good thing she'd done. Another good thing for me. And just before heading out for the store I thought, *Maybe Honor in her messed up ways is doin' somethin' right in this world after all.* I sure hoped she could see it that way.

Honor

I awoke to a familiar yet foreign face. Stern brown eyes and tight white curls framing a dark face layered with years of wisdom. It was like seeing my fairy godmother standing there, breathing her light down on me. Knowing Blondell was near made me feel safe—it reminded me of how I used to feel when Daddy was around.

Until I saw what she was holding.

My eyes bugged at the sight of a glass of thick red liquid. Blondell's eyes were closed, and she seemed to be praying while swirling it around and around in her gnarled hand. "Duchess tol' me 'bout yo fallin' out," she said finally. "Got low blood. Got ta build it up. Ya, drink dis."

"I'm not drinking that!" I squealed, shooting up to sitting and covering my mouth with my pillow. Blondell didn't bat an eyelash.

"Ain blood, gal, iz beet. Beet jewz."

I relaxed a little but still didn't want to drink it.

"Gw'on, On'ry. Ain gwine bite. Hurr'yup now."

I grabbed the glass and stuck it to my lips, but before I could sip it she added, "Don' gib me no t'anks when you done now, ya? Ain gwine work if ya do."

"Oh, okay." I drank the stuff like a shot of tequila—don't breathe, don't open your nose, just throw it down and get it over with.

"Mm hmm," she muttered when I handed her the glass, careful *not* to thank her for it.

Now sitting, my eyes fell on a large, oval sweetgrass basket Blondell must have brought with her. Heaven was spilling out of it onto the rug. My easel, paints, and canvases were piled neatly there behind her. Tears formed when I saw my things, and I slid out of bed, forgetting everything else. I had my paints back! I bent down to touch it all.

"Did you bring these? Have you had this stuff? I've been wondering what happened to it!" I leaned over and hugged Blondell, careful again not to thank her. I could feel the fragile bones of her rib cage in her back. She stiffened and tried to smile. Such a proud woman, I could tell it wasn't often she allowed her teeth to show.

I picked up my brushes and counted them. Each one was there, even the two scrawny ones that came with my 1950s paint-by-numbers set that Daddy had gotten me at a garage sale. Why in the world he'd thought half-painted Mexican donkeys and ballerinas were appropriate for a girl turning sixteen years old, I'll never know. He'd tried anyway. I'd ditched those paintings years ago—it turned out not "every man was a Rembrandt" after all—but I'd held on to those brushes for three tumultuous decades, through marriage and divorce, big hair and disco.

The last time I'd seen them was, well, the night in the park when I took all those pills. What a horrid night. I remembered bringing all of my art supplies with me to the bench. A sort of sacrificial offering perhaps? Something to go with me to the afterworld? Either that or I just wanted some kind, creative person to step over my dead body, take them, and give my things a good home. Now I knew Miss Blondell had been saving them for me all along. What an unexpected blessing.

"Ah'tis' need ta paint," she said, nodding at me, reading me. "Paint dis, paint dat, paint eb'ry'ting you can git yo hand on, On'ry. Dat's yo remedy. Got ta paint yo way to well."

I was feeling better already, beet juice or not. I realized that yes, I was an artist—perhaps not a great one, but an artist nonetheless. Artists make art. Without it, I had nothing. I needed my paints to lose myself in them. That's when artists are happiest—when we've lost ourselves completely in something else.

Too many times I used a man as my canvas, trying to fix him, change him, figure him out. My ex, Jack, was my canvas, and I gave myself over to him—not that he ever wanted that much of me. After we married, my soul disappeared, and only a shadow of Honor was left behind, skulking around the house, waiting for him to make my next move. I'm positive that's part of the reason we divorced. Not all of it, but a part, for sure. At the ripe old age of twenty-three I was so willing to lose myself completely in him that after a while, Jack was married to nobody at all.

Anyway, I digress—Blondell had given me the one thing that could cheer my spirits—I had my paints back. And the best thing about it was, I hadn't the slightest inclination to create a self-portrait. Hallelujah! I didn't want to paint myself again for the rest of my life.

I wondered where the painting was I'd done that night at the playground. I looked at Blondell and it was uncanny, as if she was watching the workings of my mind. She shook her head.

"Trew ya paintin' away," she said. "You ain need no remindah ob dat mess. You gettin' bettah, Miss On'ry. Ya blood buildin' up. Ya heart cleanin' on out."

I was so grateful to her I didn't know what to do. I tried to convey with my eyes exactly what she was becoming to me. But in a way, it was almost like having Mother back. I had a yearning to please her, a reverence for her, but also a strong will to pull away and rebel like heck against her. Do you imagine we re-create all of our relationships with people? Looking back I can see my pattern. With Brett I recreated my relationship with Jack, and with Jack it was someone before that. Daddy.

Duchess

Ah yes. There's something about little girls and their daddies. My daddy, like I said, was poor not only in cash but in spirit. He was depressed all the time and never spoke to me much. But I was his only child. It hurt me so bad that I wanted nothing to do with Daddy because of it. Or maybe it made me need him more, I don't know. All I know is Mackey was Daddy's complete and polar opposite, and that's exactly why I married him. Against Mama's better judgment.

If I had it to do all over again, I'd handcuff Mama to my arm and haul her through my whole life, obeying every rule she set for me. I know I wouldn't be where I am today if I'd listened to her years ago. How's that for regret? It's a shame we only see things clearly in hindsight. God really should do something about that.

17

July 31, 2006

Duchess

My arms were dusted white with flour when Honor surprised me in the kitchen. I was mixing up a storm. I smiled at her and said, "I'm making you some more of my mama's homemade buttermilk biscuits. Can't you just taste 'em? Goodness, we had 'em every Sunday for supper. I'd always split mine down the middle and smother it in fresh cream butter and this wonderful honey Mr. Hatchell used to bring us from his beehives. Oh, Mama, Mama, Mama."

My hand sank through the dough when my mind wandered off to yesteryear. Honor cleared her throat to reel me back in.

"Goodness, I do miss her. I sure would love for her to be here," I said finally, wadding my dough up again with more flour. "Oh, and she'd love you, Honor. You feelin' any better? You got more color to you, that's for sure."

"Much better," she said. "And hungry now. What can I do to help?"

"Not a thing."

"I have to do something!" She picked up a carton of eggs and looked around for a bowl to crack them in.

"Not in my kitchen you don't! Not today. You're *my* guest this mornin'. Just sit your skinny self down, dear, and let Saint Anne put some meat on you. Just look at me," I said, wiggling my skirt-covered hips, "I know what I'm doin'."

Honor put the eggs down and I grabbed them. "I must say, I got my work cut out for me. Why, the looks of you, you're skinnier than a chicken in wintertime!"

"You think I'm skinny?" she asked. "Really?"

"Well, just look at you! I could pick my teeth with you after breakfast!"

A little smile spread across her lips. "How about that. You know, I've tried all my life to lose weight. Not that I was ever really that big—but my rear-end, you know."

"Oh, child, you don't know the meaning of 'rear-end.' Turn around. Show me. Where is it? Who took it?"

"Hmm. It used to be here, I promise," she said. "Strange. Must be stress, I suppose."

Honor walked to the window and stared out over the ocean. Her eyes fell to the mound of shells where I keep my painful memories. I keep them close to me, see, at all times. But there I was, cooking a feast for her and loving every second of it. Not a care in the world, past, present, or future, when my hands are full.

I wrapped an apron around my waist. I was wearing clothes, a peasant skirt and a way-too-tight tank top that showed my long, sagging cleavage. It used to fit me just fine, and I couldn't understand what had happened.

"You look very nice today," Honor teased me. "Thank you, thank you, *thank you* for going *clothed* for breakfast."

"Well now, I take offense to that, young lady! Why in the world would you prefer these rags over my naturally svelte and beautiful body? Aren't you used to me by now?"

Honor laughed and said, "Well, I don't know. I could probably be here for twenty years and never get used to you being naked. God help me the day your nudity doesn't shock the dickens out of me."

"Hmmph." I shook my head. "Some folks are just prudes, I reckon."

The biscuits were in the oven now, smelling like heaven on earth, and I was frying some ham in a skillet.

"I haven't had country ham in years," Honor said, leaning her elbows on the island. "Not since we used to visit Grandmama. I loved going to Grandmama's house, playing tag down by the lake, riding horses in her field. We had this little yellow pony named Peanut. I loved that sweet thing. Oh, how I cried when he passed away."

"I'm so sorry, dear."

"But poor Alice! She's the one who found him. I don't know how she stood it, but then again, she's always been so incredibly strong—tucking her pain in her pockets and simply moving on."

We talked a little more about Alice and her daughters too—Honor sure was smitten with those girls—while we feasted on the back porch overlooking the ocean. We'd brought out plates, silver, cloth napkins, cut flowers in a vase—the works.

"This is the nicest meal I can remember," Honor said as we finished up. "Here. Let me get those."

"Nothin' doin'," I told her. "You put those dishes down this minute."

"But you made the meal. Please let me clean up."

"Honor Maddox," I warned, giving her my mama's evil eye. I knew she wasn't feeling well still. Didn't look good, neither—sort of yellowish, or green even. "You just rest now," I told her. "Can't have you gettin' sick on us again, now, can we?"

Honor

Not one to look a gift horse in the mouth, I set my dishes down in the sink and then left for the study. I'd wanted to go in there ever since cleaning it spotless. Wisdom and adventure covered the walls, there for the finding. Dark wood shelves from floor to ceiling were lined with books. You would have thought you'd died and gone to heaven, Alice, if you saw it—the way you love to read.

There was a cozy floral chair in the corner by the window, covered in a soft afghan. It was calling my name. I looked along the shelves, hoping to find a book that spoke to me just as loudly. But most of what I saw was political or financial in nature, most definitely the Duchess' late husband's—until I came across a row of tawdry romance novels with long-haired, bare-chested men embracing sexy, bosomy women. Really not my thing. But tucked in the middle of them all was a book called *Miracles of the Patron Saint Anne*. Relieved to find something that interested me, I grabbed it and settled into the chair, tucking my feet up under me.

I read for a while with the breeze blowing gently against the window, and then I stopped. I couldn't believe what I found in that book.

I got up slowly—my stomach was tender again—and went back into the kitchen to share it with Duchess. She was leaning over the counter, wiping up her spills, her face beaming with pride.

"You won't believe what I learned in here," I said, holding the book up for her. "Did you know St. Anne is considered the grandmother of Jesus, Mary's mother? Have you ever heard that? With my Baptist upbringing, I sure hadn't."

"Why no dear, I—"

"She's also the Catholic patron saint of—get this—mothers, grandmothers, and *childless people*! Can you believe it? What irony! And here we both are having found our way to her island."

"Hmm. How 'bout that," Duchess said.

"You know, maybe we're both here for a reason. Maybe this is the place we were both supposed to wind up. Imagine that."

"Yes. Imagine that."

I closed the book and walked to the window. Watching the tide roll in, I was struck suddenly by my good fortune. I'm suicidal one day, then cared for and given a lovely home on the ocean with a view people would kill for the next. Yet here I was. It was the first time in many years I felt the hand of God in my life. With all I'd done to destroy it so far, He'd sheltered me and provided for me. Hadn't He? My heart lifted to my throat with that realization. I'd been so distant from God for so long—*so* distant—that sitting in that kitchen with Duchess, feeling His breath on my shoulder, just turned me to jelly.

But jelly turned to ill again.

I excused myself and tried to make it back to my bedroom, but got sick on the way, thankfully only on the hardwoods and not the rugs we'd worked so hard on. Duchess was still in the kitchen, oblivious. I could hear her humming happily while pots clanked and water splashed in the sink. I cleaned up my tracks and stumbled to the bedroom. Passing my beautiful paints and canvases on the floor, I longed to play with them. I knew they would have to wait.

I continued to get sick the rest of that day. Had it not been for the obvious concern of the Duchess, I would have sworn she'd poisoned me with her breakfast and "all the trimmin's."

The day was the thirty-first of July. Looking back, that's the first time I can see there was something truly wrong with me. I only wish I'd realized it then.

18

Alice

The dying person may begin to detach from the world, often sleeping more and talking less. This is the beginning of letting go.

I'm so tired. I've been at the hospital for over forty-eight hours. I haven't showered, haven't slept much. I simply read Honor's letters and sit by her side. And I pray for a miracle. At one point, I flip through the television channels and find an evangelist who claims to heal people. What a crock. I do just as he says, I hold her up in my mind, in my heart. I lay Honor before

Him and pray to God as hard as I can. Nothing miraculous happens. Nothing at all.

Then my cell phone rings. It's Melody.

"Hi, Mom. How is she?"

"The same."

"Oh. I'm sorry. Well, um, we're making a good dinner tonight. Seafood lasagna and French bread. And salad. Oh, and we got you some good wine too. Red. I told Dad he has to wait to open it till you get here."

I smile. I miss my girls.

"You think you could come home?" she asks. "Just for a little while?"

I look at Honor. She hasn't changed—hasn't moved a muscle, hasn't improved or declined. I'm exhausted and desperately need a bath. I'm hungry, out of sorts. Hopeless. I need my girls.

"Sure. Tell Dad to come get me."

We hang up and I breathe in deeply. I feel torn between the living and the dying. At this stage, I'm not sure which category I belong to.

Saying that leaving Honor is "difficult" just doesn't do it justice. It's nearly impossible for me to break free. I press my lips against her forehead and listen to her shallow breathing. I promise her I'll be back soon and pray for nothing to happen to her while I'm gone. I don't think I could handle that.

Wayne helps me to the truck and lifts me inside. The door slams cool air against my face and I'm grateful for it. I don't speak on the way home, and Wayne doesn't ask me any questions. I'm grateful also for the silence.

The girls are beaming at me as I hobble in the door. There's a fire roaring in the fireplace, something smells wonderful from the kitchen, and the warm glow of familiarity cradles me from the second my good foot hits the floor. It's wonderful to be home, but my heart isn't in it. I keep thinking of Honor. She's been with me every Christmas that I can remember. Even the one year she didn't think she could make it, there she came, Brett in tow at the last minute. I remember she was crying when she walked in. She couldn't bear being away from "her girls" for the holidays.

Standing here, looking at my nice clean house, the nativity scene on the mantel, the candles lit on the table, I understand why so many people hate the holidays. They only amplify the emptiness you feel if someone you love is missing.

The Christmas tree is glittering and sheltering presents—some new ones, too, either from the girls or Wayne. They have to be from the girls though. Wayne never bought a present in his life. It's always been my job to play Santa or the Tooth Fairy or anything that requires faith and imagination.

"Why don't you take a bath before dinner," suggests Melody, pragmatic as usual. It's the best prospect I've had in days.

I can hear Christmas carols playing on the stereo downstairs. Wayne is singing, which means he's somewhere between having a couple drinks and becoming fully snockered. I know I should get out of the bath and go down for dinner soon before he crosses the line between man and monster. We've watched him cross it so many times before.

I feel somewhat human again in my bathrobe and slipper. The other foot is decked in my new ugly blue shoe. Sarah hands me a glass of merlot, and I sip it like it's pure gold. The warmth travels through my veins like life-giving elixir.

That's when Beethoven begins playing again. I scramble for my purse and pull the phone out. The caller ID shows *Waccamaw Hosp*, and my heart lurches.

"Hello!" I say frantically.

"This is Charlene from . . ."

"Is Honor okay? What's wrong?"

"Is this Alice Chandler?"

"Yes!"

"Your sister, Honor. She's awake. I thought you'd like to know."

"She's awake!" I scream and jump up, forgetting that my foot is broken. I tumble onto the floor, my robe flaying open, showing my skinny white legs.

"She's awake! She's awake!" I'm crying when my girls pull me up. Sarah looks at me excitedly. "Go on, get dressed! Hurry, hurry!"

"I'm sorry, honey," I say to Melody. "Everything smells wonderful . . ."

"Mother, go on! She's awake!" The girls help me up the stairs and the next bit flies by. In minutes I'm dressed with overnight bag in hand. Wayne sulks, but he doesn't say anything because the girls are in the truck with us. He always tries to be on his best behavior around them. We're all squeezed in together like sardines, the air is cold and harsh, and my heart pounds with relief and panic. She's awake. Thank God!

My baby sister is awake.

19

St. Anne's Isle
August 1, 2006

Honor

I can see it so clearly right now—the first painting I did for Duchess was just two days after my sweet reunion with my brushes and paints. It was a pink whelk shell that filled the entire sixteen-by-twenty-four-inch canvas with sexy, rounded edges leading to a mysterious dark cavern in the middle. It was the same shell I'd passed on to her from Blondell.

I painted it first thing in the morning when warm light filled the room with golden hues—from memory too—something I rarely did, having always felt the need to rely on actual objects for inspiration. I thought if it wasn't right there in front of me, I'd lose any sense of realism. And without realism, what in the world did you have? But when I painted that first enormous shell, I did away with all that. I broke the rules. I used broad stokes with a wide brush. My colors were vivid, my right arm wild. To be honest, I can hardly remember painting that picture—it seemed to flow out of me like the inevitable evening tide. I knew one thing for sure when I set it at one end of the bedroom and peeked at it from the other side—I was *alive*. I loved that feeling. My painting gave that to me—it was truly a gift.

I'd been struggling to like Duchess, wavering back and forth. She had this annoying way of grinding her teeth when she thought no one else could hear, and she overdid every single word to me in this Southern drawl. Don't get me wrong, I'm as Southern as the rest, but there's a point at which an accent is used, not for the inability to speak otherwise, but simply for dramatic effect. And I had to build up my gastrointestinal fortitude when browsing the house for fear I'd find her—well, you know. Literally, it makes me gag to this day to think about it. I have never been one to gawk at or study my own naked body, much less some strange old woman's.

I knew for a fact that Duchess wasn't playing with a full deck, but this was my task that God and Blondell had given me: like her or leave her. I sure as heck didn't have anywhere else to go, and in a strange way, she was growing on me.

When I decided to paint again (and it would *not* be my own

face), I closed my eyes and tried to think nice thoughts about Duchess. I asked God to put in my mind what would help her most. That silly pink conch shell came to me instantly.

Duchess

I nearly fell over when I saw what Honor had done.

"You painted that?" I was clutching my bare bosom and ran off spouting, "Let me go get my glasses. Hold on. Don't go anywhere! Just let me get my glasses!"

I could feel my fanny wiggling all the way down the hall like Jell-O on a pie plate, and I just had to laugh. I came back to find her sitting on the sofa with the painting propped next to her on the floor. I was wearing my beige floor-length shift just for her and had my bifocals perched way south on my nose. I sat real close and gave her a bug-eyed look and then picked up the canvas, checking my fingers to make sure the paint was dry. The smell of paint mixed with my wrinkled linen was clean and fresh, just wonderful.

"This is *gor*-geous, Honor! I cannot believe you did this. *You* did this? How'd you learn to paint like this? You are so unbelievably talented! I simply cannot believe I have such a talented artist residin' under my very own roof!"

"It wasn't much," she said. "I just thought you might like it."

I gasped, and my glasses fell to my chest, dangling from a beaded necklace.

"This is for me? No. Are you serious? You painted this for—
me?" My voice caught in the back of my throat, and I was about
to let loose. Sweet child.

"Let's go see where we can put it. You want to?" she asked,
standing up quickly and grabbing it from me before my tears
could fall.

Honor and I wandered from the living room to the kitchen.
We found some bare walls where it would have fit but kept on
moving. We made it to my bedroom, everything all white and
crisp now. The floor, curtains, walls, loveseat, everything was
white—at least it was after we'd cleaned it all. When Honor first
saw my room it was covered in knickknacks and clothes all over
the floor, bed linens unmade—the works. Looked like a teenager
lived here, unhappy with how her clothes fit, never satisfied,
never able to keep order. It's the way the inside of my head gets
at times, just showing on the outside, I reckon.

"This is perfect!" I told her, holding the painting up in the
hallway outside my bathroom. "I can lie in bed and see it from
there. And it might just give me reason to go in my closet a little
more." I elbowed her and grinned, showing my sense of humor. I
knew wearing no clothes was odd. I knew it, but for some reason
I just couldn't stop walking around, waggling my ample thighs
and sharing my pale whiteness with the world and God Almighty.

Honor saw me grinning from ear to ear, and she had to smile
too. I stood back from her painting, saying over and over, "I love
it. I just love it."

Honor stood over my shoulder as I studied every brush stroke. This was her offering to me and the babies I'd lost. Truly, it was the nicest thing anybody'd ever done for me.

Honor

I became something in the moments Duchess was engrossed in my work. I became *something*. I can't put it any clearer. I realized the only time I was *anything* was when I left my colorful marks in the world.

I was grateful for that—for my ability to become.

And I painted another shell for her, at her request. This one was the same size canvas, but it was a bivalve—not a clam, not an oyster, but one of those tiny butterfly shells you find with holes in the end where the creature has escaped—gone on to something bigger and better no doubt.

It was in blues, this one. Duchess *ooooohed* when she saw it. I must say, I did too. It was a complete and utter surprise when it came out of me, my right hand moving with unearthly speed while my left hand stayed steady, holding the water-like hues. It was an otherworldly and beautiful experience. My painting was evolving into something much different than ever before. I was painting for Duchess, but also for myself, and also it seemed, for something bigger than both of us.

We hung that painting on the wall of the study, in the little nook where the cozy chair is, so we could look at it while gathering thoughts and watching the ocean—or reading and getting lost in other people's lives.

August 15, 2006

After nearly two weeks of furious creation, my shells made appearances all over the house. There were a dozen or more now. My fingers, my mind, my soul thought of nothing more than creating those dad-gum shells. I'd walk the beach in the early mornings before Duchess ever woke, scouring for new inspiration. It was hard sometimes because the Sea Island beaches are not like they were near Murrells Inlet growing up. The shells on St. Anne's are ground to a pulp, and it's a rarity to find one intact. Life, the ocean, beats the cream out of them, and the ones that survive are truly remarkable.

Duchess approached me one afternoon, wearing a tiny white halter-top with a long, colorful sarong skirt. Her stomach rolled down over her waistline, leaving a ring like Jupiter, orbiting her middle. "I'd say we have enough for a showin', don't you think?" she announced. "I'm invitin' absolutely everyone I know—and that means practically the entire island—to come view Honor's Spectacular Sea Shells. Doesn't that sound wonderful?"

"You're what? No you're not. Really?"

"Of course, dear! Why not?" She put her hands on her hips. "It'll give me an excuse to throw one of my fabulous parties. You don't know it, but I used to be quite fashionable and known for my swanky soirees. And your paintin's, Miss Honor, are worth shoutin' about. Screamin' about! I just have to show off to the entire island that I am close, no, *best* friends with the famous artist, Honor Maddox."

I was flabbergasted. Terrified. Excited at the same time. Crazy here, apparently my best friend now, wanted to throw me a party. No one had ever thrown me a party. I was a nobody, a do-no-gooder, a do-nothing. I was going to be the *artiste*, the one who everyone goggled over. At least, that's what I envisioned while lying in bed, dreaming about it. In those long, lingering few weeks to follow I would paint and eat and sleep and take my lessons from Blondell and the Gullah nannies. Every now and again when my nerves got the best of me, I would crawl into the bathroom and throw up.

But I have to say, despite not feeling well, I was growing happier than I'd ever been in my life—except for when I was with you, Alice. My endeavors on St. Anne's were becoming worthy of you, minus the lying, that is. I wish now I hadn't lied to you about why I'd moved to a nicer home—or why I'd taken in a crazy old roommate. How I wish I hadn't lied to you—and to myself—about so many things.

20

September 9, 2006

Honor

I'd been staying with Duchess for over a month now, and I'd never seen her so excited. She'd been fully dressed for days, much to my relief, and running around the house with an actual purpose. She had scribbled handwritten notes on some old stationery, inviting all the islanders to *St. Anne's Gallery—A Showing for Renowned Artist Honor Maddox*. I was tickled beyond belief. What was the worst that could happen? I didn't know these people, not really. If it was a complete flop, Duchess would be the one looking silly, what with her crazy reputation and all. I would simply fess up to the fact that I only "dabble" in paints, and that's it. *She simply insisted on showing these silly little paintings. You know how she is.* I recited my speech in my head.

One evening, the two of us, decked out in sweat pants and T-shirts with full round glasses of cabernet in our hands, mounted her little (pink, of course) golf cart and headed out into the night. St. Anne's has more golf carts than cars, actually. If you have to walk more than a mile, a golf cart will do just fine, thank you very much. My Jetta, still at the playground, had sat idle for months, as had Duchess' Cadillac, hibernating beneath her raised house. The only time anyone used a car was to leave the island to cross the waterway to the mainland—something true islanders never did unless heading to Savannah, Beaufort, or Charleston.

My skin pricked alive under the sultry wash of evening air as we stole quietly through sleepy neighborhoods, slipping notes into mailboxes. More than a few times, dogs barked at us, causing lights to flick on in houses and us to giggle and speed away like teenaged bandits. I must say, it was a ball. We left a trail of invitations all over St. Anne's from the ritziest mansions on the beach to the shanties of Gullah natives painted blue to keep the haints and hags out.

"Haints are the spirits of the dead that still roam among us," Duchess explained. "But a hag, so I've been told, is an old woman who can shed her skin at night." The air around me froze still, and the sky grew even darker. "She haunts people, finding them in their beds asleep." Her voice grew to a hush.

"Then she rides on their chest all night long till they can't breathe anymore."

I didn't say anything. I couldn't say anything. Was this true? Who was to say? All I know is my skin crawled as we passed though a white cloud of mist hovering over the warm ground.

"You'll find there are things that the Gullahs do to keep hags out of their houses. Haint blue paint is one for sure, but you remember Miss Blondell's house? Remember how she has those brooms outside her doors? Honey, that ain't 'cause she's so clean and proper. No, she believes a hag'll have to stop and count each and every piece of straw before comin' into her room at night."

"Really," I said.

"That's the honest-to-goodness truth. Said she got 'rode' once and wasn't about to let that ever happen again."

"Well, I'll be."

Things quieted down after that. I felt more reverence for the evening, for the islanders, for the ghosts swirling around us. Plus, we were getting tired. Our wine was long gone, and we were finishing up our delivery.

We headed back to the house and struggled up the stairs. I was grateful to be back. Duchess had a good twenty years and thirty pounds on me, but on this night, I was the one having a hard time with heavy legs. I was exhausted. Before we opened the front door, I touched Duchess' arm and said, "Thank you."

She looked in my eyes and then grabbed my chin and squeezed. "You are so welcome, Honor dear. Now come on in here and get you some rest. We got a big day ahead of us."

The door shut behind me, leaving the world outside. And the floor beneath me, the furniture in front of me, all of it, I realized then, felt like coming home.

Duchess

"*I'd like to paint your wall,*" *Honor told me the next morn*-ing, sneaking up on me with a cup of black coffee. I was sunning nude on the porch. I cracked my eyelids and saw how the yellow glare from the sun shimmered off my pale skin, giving my body a strange glow like chicken breasts under a heat lamp.

"You'd like to paint my what?" I asked, holding my hand up to shield the sun. I peeked at her through one eye.

"Your wall. Or walls. Whichever one you want." She sat down on the porch boards beside me and faced the ocean, leaning up against my chaise. My body was settled like warm pudding into the creases of that lounge chair. I felt so heavy I pictured God needing a great big spatula to flip me over, leaving my behind covered in thick grill stripes.

"My walls?"

"I'm out of canvases, Anne. Sad, but true. I really could use something to paint."

"Well, I can get you more—"

"No, no. I do not want you buying canvases for me. You've done quite enough as it is. And the showing is just a couple weeks away, I—please. I would like to do this for you. Plus, I have a great idea for the dining room wall."

Honor grinned like the Cheshire cat, and I knew she wanted to do this. I scrambled for a striped beach towel to cover my privates.

"Well, I—I had that room painted special for me, you know. It might just break his heart if you go in there and cover it up. Sonny's heart, I mean."

"Oh," she said, dejected.

"Oh, who am I kiddin'?" I heaved a long sigh. "That boy'll never set foot in here again. Not after that last time, that's for sure."

"What? Oh, you have got to tell me about this," she pried. "What happened last time? What?"

"Well, if you must know"—I pulled up to sitting and the chaise groaned beneath me—"I had invited Sonny up for a glass of iced tea after I had him trimmin' my bushes . . . if you know what I mean."

I said that last part in a low, seductive purr, and my eyebrows arched with the implication.

"Really?" she asked.

"No, no. I'm just kiddin'. Sonny really was trimmin' my ligustrums out front. And doin' my lawn, but nothin' more. Nothin' more. What a shame." I gave her a sly smile. "But when he was through, like I said, he came in, I gave him sweet tea, he said

172

'Thank you ma'am,' and then I grabbed his little tushie and maybe goosed him a little . . ."

"You didn't!" Honor squealed, covering her mouth. "You are so bad!"

"Honey, you should have seen the look on that poor boy's face! Like he'd been bit by a moccasin. His cheeks went all white and red and then all purple—poor thing must never have been with a woman is all I can figure. He *is* right young still—twenties or thirties—can't tell. Anyway, so you go on and paint that room chartreuse for all I care, Honor. Sonny and his sweet cheeks, sadly, won't be comin' to call on Saint Anne anytime soon, I'm afraid. Unless he comes to the party . . . no, I don't think he will. You go on and do what you need to do, dear."

And that's just how it started—the beginning of Honor's beautiful new relationship. With my walls.

My dining room is a large massive cell, imposing in size and propped up with four white columns on one side. The view is to die for, perched on the edge of the ocean, right next to the porch. There's a gorgeous Persian rug, my mother-in-law's, in warm toffees and creams on the floor, but the walls at that time, sad to say, were pastel pink—a most unappetizing color.

Honor and I had not sat in this room for a meal yet. Mostly because, to me, it felt too large and formal. I preferred the intimate porch instead of the heavy, carved mahogany table and chairs. But Honor wanted to sit in that dining room. Said it deserved to have meals taken in it, deserved to be *oohed* and *aahed* over. And for what I'd done for her so far, Honor said I deserved that very same treatment. Breaks my heart thinking about it.

She hauled out some old white drop sheets from my closet. I helped her push the table to one side, and we laid those sheets down on the floor. Honor was so excited, jibber-jabbering, hands shaking, until—

"How could I be so stupid!" she wailed, staring down at her art supplies.

"What's wrong, dear?"

"This is such a big space. How could I have missed this?" she whimpered. "What was I thinking?" Honor sat down right there on the floor and her bottom lip plumped up. Her eyelids pinched and then tears started to fall. "I'm so stupid."

"Stupid, honey? For what?" I reached my arm around her and stroked her back, comforting her the way my mama used to do me.

"I don't have enough paint," she admitted like a child through sobs. Helpless.

"Paint? Is that all? Well, heavens, Honor. I sure as heck do! Let's run on down in the garage. You know how many times I've colored these walls? This entire house?" Her crying eased like a faucet turning off in her head. When she realized I was serious, she gave me her full attention.

"Let's see. There was the blue period," I told her, "after Fluffy died and I was mournin' just like, what's that fella's name? Picasso." I stepped over the dropcloths and headed for the hallway, beckoning for her to follow.

"Then there was my peach phase. I was drinking way too much schnapps in those days. Oh goodness!" I tiptoed 'cross the floor, careful to keep my robe in place. I tied it tighter just to be sure. Didn't want to upset her then. "Oh, and yes, the dreadful green phase didn't last too long—it just added to my depression," I whispered like telling her something she didn't already know.

I stopped in the foyer and swept my arm out proudly displaying the home around me. "I just recently entered a pleasant pink phase—it's my time to dream and pamper myself, you see. I switch colors more than leaves in fall, honey! You just won't believe your pretty eyes when you see the stash of paint waitin' for you down there."

And I wasn't lying. Paint cans were stacked all over this little six-by-eight-foot room under the house. I had to undo padlocks to get in there, for good reason. Thefts are extremely rare on St. Anne's Isle—everybody knows it—but I can't take the chance of something special getting stolen. I never even lock my front door, so I could tell Honor was wondering what it was all about—the locks, I mean. She figured it out soon enough though.

There was sweet Fluffy, God rest her soul, stuffed in the corner. It doesn't look like my Fluffy anymore though, not really. Looks scary now because they botched her all up, hair all this way and that and crazy eyes that don't look a thing like her. Just looks like one of those scary critters on the wall of the Bates Motel in *Psycho*. I just never had the heart to get rid of Fluffy, but

I can't bring her into the house looking like that neither. Just a bad situation all around.

Honor never even mentioned Fluffy, though she couldn't have missed her. Her mind was reeling with ideas for the mural. She'd never done anything on so grand a scale before. And lucky for me, I was a voluptuous guinea pig with just the right size wall.

21

Alice

At times, a dying person may suddenly appear well. This does not mean there will be recovery. Take this opportunity to say what you need to say and have closure.

I ask the girls and Wayne to stay in the waiting room while I go in to see Honor alone. My stomach is spinning, excited to see her awake finally and dreading it at the same time. I'm hoping to see my baby sister as I remember her, but I realize I may be setting myself up for a fall.

She's sitting up a little more than the last time I saw her. She's waiting for me, I can tell by the look in her eyes though they're bloodshot and her irises are more gray than blue. Honor forces a little smile when I hop to her side.

"What happened to you?" she asks weakly, looking at my crutches.

"What happened to *you*?" I say, attempting lightness.

"I'm so sorry," Honor says.

"Shhhh," I tell her, bending down to hug her. I clutch her hand and lay my head in her hair. I breathe her in deeply and my eyes begin to fill. I whisper in her ear, "I'm so sorry. I'm sorry I wasn't here for you."

My body begins to tremble so I straighten up and wheel a chair to the side of her bed, never letting go of her hand.

"I should have told you," she says slowly, each word an effort. "I'm so stupid."

"You are not stupid!" I hiss. "Don't say that! You're my sister. I love you! I'll do anything for you. Anything. You hear that? I'm not leaving your side again. I'm not going anywhere."

Honor struggles with her mouth, and I grab the cup of water next to her and put the straw up to her lips. It's all she can do to draw any up, so I bring it back and put my finger on the end of the straw like I used to do for my baby girls. I put the other end to her lips and let the water slide onto her parched tongue. Water dribbles down her chin, and I grope for a towel nearby and dry her neck. We stay silent for a few moments. Then she looks at me, and I see fear cloud her eyes.

"I'm not going to make it," she says as if she's just found out. "I'm really going to die."

I stare at her for a long time, unable to move, unable to respond. I am frozen. My spirit is trying desperately to leave me, to leave the room. Finally, I say, "It's okay, honey. I'm going to be here with you every second. I promise!"

"Don't cry," she says as I grab for a tissue and blot my face. Honor blinks and a tear falls down her cheek. I wipe it away, then stand and face the window. It's dark, and by the streetlights I can see it's beginning to snow again. Suddenly, I am miserably cold.

"I don't know what to say," I admit, turning back to face her. "I just wish you had told me. No. I'm sorry. I promised myself I wouldn't do this. What matters is I'm here now and you're awake." I force a smile. "I've been reading your memoir, you know."

"Really?" She almost beams.

"Yep. It's some of your best work."

"You think so?" Her voice is scratchy. "Maybe I should find a publisher." The right side of her mouth tilts up. I move over to her and give her another straw-full of water.

"How far along are you?" she asks after a labored swallow.

"You're getting ready to paint that dining room. Oh, and you've already met the cute Officer Simmons."

"He is so cute."

"And you're trying to figure out the Duchess. Are these folks real, Honor? I've never heard of such people. And she really walks around naked?"

"I kid you not," she says. Then her eyes close.

"Honor?" She doesn't say anything. I look over at the heart monitor to make sure she's all right. "Honor? Please don't go. Are you sleeping? Honor?"

Honor slips away again, either to sleep or into a coma, I don't know which. It's all I can take. I lean over and cry then, burying my face in her hand. For a brief moment, I had my Honor back. It felt just like it always did. But now she's gone, and the emptiness is even worse than before she woke up. I didn't tell her everything I needed to. *I need more time. We need more time together!*

I sob louder and harder than ever before in my life, and I don't hear when my family walks in the door. My girls touch my back and my hair, and they kneel down and cry right along with me. Wayne just stands back and watches it all.

22

St. Anne's Isle
September 10, 2006

Honor

There she was again, rifling through her bookshelf in the study—in the nude. I tried not to let her see me and started backing away, but Duchess heard me anyway.

"Oh, there you are. Can you reach that up there, Honor? I can't get that cookbook there. The red and white one, you see it? Yes, that's it. The Betty Crocker one."

I handed it to her.

"Goodness, the memories. This was my mama's favorite, you know. See how worn the edges are? How 'bout you grab a book and sit here with me? We can read for a while."

"Oh no," I told her. "I just need this one book." I reached up and grabbed one. "I'm just going to take this into the dining room and study it for a little inspiration. Then I'll see you in a little bit. Okay?"

She nodded, looking slightly dejected, and I walked away, finally connecting the dots. Like it or not, I was beginning to understand the Duchess. It seemed to me her biggest desire was the same as my own: to be known, in and out, to be naked in the eyes of others and to be loved through and through in spite of it all. Don't we all need that? Duchess wanted so badly to be naked—figuratively speaking, that is—to bare her soul to the world and to shout, *Look at me! I am beautiful!* Only problem is, Duchess took the baring part too literally.

Do you remember when we were girls, Alice, that television show we used to watch with that funny little man who painted "happy little trees"? We were mesmerized each time we watched him paint mountains in minutes. Immediately following the show we would put our brushes up to white paper, waiting for the magic to begin. He always made it look so easy, but when we tried it ourselves, the mountains turned out sloppy and our trees certainly were not happy. We would go from elation to depression in about five minutes.

Well, when I set out to paint Duchess' dining room wall, I actually became like the" happy little tree" man. Life and colors flowed from my wrist like magic. I danced along the wall making broad strokes, painting larger than life. I don't even remember doing it, quite honestly. I was completely lost in the act of creation. It felt spiritual or religious, as if I'd just been to church.

The whole wall only took me four or five hours to paint. It was rough at that time with details still to add in, but when I stood back and eyed it, oh my goodness. There it was. My vision had come together.

I had grabbed a book of classical art from the Duchess' library and studied it. Then I closed the book and from memory, painted Botticelli's *The Birth of Venus*.

In my version, Duchess was Venus.

She was emerging from a large seashell, nude although much thinner—I used my creative license on that—but her face was Duchess through and through. I kept her sweet eyes and rounded cheeks, her delicate small nose and animated lips. Her hair was long and blonde, almost white, flowing around her body. She was young and gorgeous, and I was humbled. I couldn't believe the work that had been done through me. That's the only way I can explain it. For once in my life, I had set myself aside to do something truly for someone else. And it turned out better than I ever could have imagined. It was haunting. It truly felt as though God had painted the Duchess beautiful *through* me.

And it was all I could do to keep her out of that room. I wouldn't allow Duchess to see it until the wall was completely finished the following afternoon.

September 11, 2006

Duchess

"Close your eyes now," Honor told me. I did, squealing like an excited child, and she led me into the dining room, her hand resting on the back of my neck. "You can open them now. Surprise."

I was stunned. My eyes darted back and forth across the wall over the cool blue water and angels in the sky. But I almost got to boo-hooing when they rested on Venus. "Oh," I breathed and grabbed my bare chest. Then I reached for a towel she'd used for clean up and tried to cover myself. With my naked behind still there for Honor and all God's creation to see, I walked forward and touched the wall, tracing my fingers over Venus' flowing hair. I was seventeen again.

"Do you like it?" Honor asked, grinning. She was a schoolgirl bringing home a string of As for Mama.

"Honor Maddox, you are . . . you're brilliant. I have never been so in awe—so proud of anyone in my whole life!" I grabbed her hand and squeezed it tight, never taking my eyes off the wall. "Mark my words, Honor. You're gonna be somebody big someday."

"Aren't you pretty?" she asked me, teasing. "You know that's you, don't you? Venus is you." I nodded, holding back tears. 'Course I knew it was me.

Finally I said, laughing, "I don't really look like that." I grabbed the towel at both ends and wrapped it tight around my body, feeling my fluff.

"No, you don't," Honor said, putting her arm around my shoulders and pulling me to her. "You're much more beautiful than that."

September 17, 2006

In the days that followed, Honor didn't paint anymore. Said she felt spent and couldn't imagine how she'd had the energy to paint that wall. She stared at it, admired it, but said somebody else must have done it—it must have just up and painted itself. And in the quiet of doing nothing creative, Honor's old self came back. It seemed anytime she had a minute to reflect, a sour poison would fill up her veins, and she'd go depressed all over again. I know the feeling.

"Don't worry about me. I'm all right," she'd say if I showed any concern. Then she'd go on up to her room again and close that blasted door. I'd listen in on the other side, worried she might try to jump off the balcony. I hid away all my pill bottles deep in my closet, too, just to be safe. I was terrified for her in those days, praying for God to send His angels to watch over her. I thought maybe she was just scared about the art show coming up. I knew she was frightened of failure and being laughed at, though it shouldn't have meant a hill of beans to her. She didn't know anybody there. Big deal. She was showing some paintings to strangers on a tiny little island. It couldn't be that bad, could it?

But when the day finally arrived, Honor spent the morning throwing up. She couldn't hold a thing down, and it got so bad, I finally rode my golf cart to the store and brought back suppositories for nausea. Let me just tell you how much Honor enjoyed that.

"Let's just cancel," she said from behind the bathroom door.

"We can't cancel, Honor! We sent out invitations. I've had people callin', sayin' they can't wait to come! And I'm makin' my mama's cucumber sandwiches!"

Honor stayed quiet.

"Is this really that important to you?" she asked me finally.

"It's only important to me because I'm so proud of you." Of course, I hoped it would do her some good.

"Let's just see if the medicine works," she said. "If I'm not better in a couple hours, will you please just stick a sign up on the door saying we changed our minds or something?"

I said yes, and she stayed close to the toilet, waiting for her insides to settle.

The first person to come to the door was Ruby. She knocked twice and then walked right in.

"Hello? Duchess? Well, hey there, Miss Honor!" she squeaked. "I come to see your paintin'."

Ruby took off the red hat that seemed to swallow her whole. She sucked in air, and her tiny mouth fell open when she saw the canvases propped up around the room. There were oyster shells and clam shells, conch shells and sand dollars, even a curly string of whelk egg sacs and a great big mermaid's purse.

"So this what you been doin', mercy me. Mercy, Lawd Jesus! Seashells and more shells. Oh, look at that. How you do all this? You go to school or somethin'? You thank you could teach me? I sure would like to paint."

Honor was getting ready to answer her when the doorbell rang. "Just a minute, Ruby."

She walked to the door, and I fixed the apron tie behind my back. I'd worked extra hard to look nice for Honor. I was wearing a real nice lavender pantsuit with my hair swept back in a socialite do, and my face was creamy with foundation. I actually wore lipstick and looked the part of the wife of a politician, well-preserved, sane. By the looks of me on this day, you'd have no idea I was anything but.

"I'll get it, Honor," I sang. "You just sit there and look pretty."

Honor looked uneasy standing, but didn't sit. She compromised by leaning against the living room chair covered in black fabric with bees all over it. I could tell she was jittery, and I just prayed the suppositories would work for a few more hours.

Blondell and Willa and the rest of the nannies started coming, and the chatter in there was getting louder and louder. Blondell hobbled with her cane from one room to the next. People were swirling around Honor on all sides like a sandstorm, praising her. "Just wonderful! Beautiful. How talented!" Honor just nodded her head and smiled.

Honor

I was thinking they were all liars. Every single one. Part of me wanted to revel in the attention. This was my moment, something I'd dreamed about my entire life. I had a room full of people who had come here just to see me and my work. They were praising me, telling me how wonderful I was. I was an artist. I was something to be admired, finally. This is what I had always craved.

Still, I thought they were lying to my face.

I imagined that when they left the house, they were going to snicker and say, "Did you see that? Can you believe she calls that art?"

I realized in that very moment that I am and have always been my own worst enemy.

Islanders began arriving by the droves. I couldn't keep them all straight.

"How do you do? So nice to see you."

"Yes, I've always loved to paint. You too? What medium?"

"Inspiration? Well, it's all around me. The island is my inspiration."

"Oh yes, I think I will paint some crabs next. What a terrific idea."

Champagne started flowing. I had a glass. Then another. I began to loosen up, and the baloney out of my mouth started flowing faster.

I was explaining to a gray-haired man in suede shoes (I immediately forgot his name) that no, I did not have any formal training, but yes, his granddaughter would absolutely love going to art school in Savannah, when I realized mid-conversation that I did not know where Blondell was.

All of a sudden I was sidetracked. One tracked. Where was Blondell? I needed to see her. I had to know what she thought of my work. I needed to know what she thought of me. I was a little girl again, hoping that Mother liked one of my drawings. I knew it was pathetic of me, but I needed her approval. I excused myself from my conversation, perhaps not so tactfully, and set out to find her.

I found Blondell in the dining room, staring at the mural of Duchess as Venus. She was rigid like a gnarled tree, tall and organic. Her walking stick seemed to be an extension of her.

There was a crowd of people around Blondell, moving, sway-ing, *oohing* and *aahing* over the mural. I felt naked myself and wanted to hide. I was completely exposed. That's when Officer Simmons touched my arm.

"Hey there, Miss Honor," he said in his low, sultry, smooth-like-black-velvet-Elvis voice. He was standing next to an older woman about half his size. "I'd like you to meet my mama. Mama? This is Honor Maddox. She's the nice lady who painted these pictures."

The lady looked up at me and smiled. "Oh, why, aren't you a pretty thing. You did this?"

I nodded and took her hand. "Why yes, I did. It's so nice to meet you." I moved around so she was facing the windows. I felt utterly self-conscious that the officer's mother was looking at a naked painting of mine. As if I was the bare one stepping out of the shell.

Out of the corner of my eye, I noticed Officer Simmons watching me. My face grew hot. He leaned in a little and whispered, "I didn't know you were this good, Miss Honor. You think you could paint me a picture sometime? Nothing like this though. No naked ladies. I mean, well—"

He blushed and looked adorable. My stomach fluttered like a million moths escaping cocoons, and I prayed I wouldn't be sick again.

"We'll see," I flirted, surprising myself.

Blondell hadn't moved. She was still staring at the mural. It unnerved me, so I touched Officer Simmons' arm to let him know I was still in the conversation, but with my other hand I reached out and touched Blondell's shoulder.

"Miss Blondell? You doing all right?"

She stayed firm. My stomach went even queasier.

I lifted my hand off of her shoulder, ashamed. Terror seized me. She hated my work! She could see I was a complete fraud! Oh, who was I kidding? I couldn't paint! I wasn't an artist! How could I be so stupid?! I wanted to just die. To throw myself off the balcony and let the ocean wash me out to sea. Just turn me into shark meat and let them clean up this waste of a life and—

Blondell slowly turned to face me.

She had a corncob pipe in her mouth. She wasn't smoking but was chewing on the end of it. She raised her hand and pulled it from her ample lips. Then she looked at me, and my whole world seemed to fall into place.

Blondell didn't say a word. Instead, her eyes were small and yellowed, and I noticed, at this moment, they were glassy. Blondell was actually tearing up. She nodded her head at me in a very small movement and grunted her approval. "Mm hmm."

That's all I needed.

I leaned in and hugged her hard and then pulled back renewed, alive. I was filled to the brim and overflowing with confidence. I was happy, truly happy, and I wished you could have been there, Alice. I made a mental note to be sure to call you that night and tell you what a success the day had been. I couldn't remember the throwing up. I couldn't remember the terror that grew like a cancer in my stomach, waiting for the guests to arrive. Or the insecurity that nearly ate me alive. All I could think about was that look in Blondell's eyes.

And it wouldn't have mattered if I hadn't sold a single piece, but I did. In fact, out of thirty canvases, I only had three of them left at the end of the day. Not that I was selling them for very much, a couple hundred dollars at the most, but people actually bought them, and now I had some cash in hand. I could buy groceries. I could buy more canvases. I could pitch in around the house and not feel like a scoundrel, leeching off of Duchess. I was proud of myself, and I'll never forget it because there have only been a handful of those days in my lifetime.

Duchess

It was eight o'clock by the time Mr. and Mrs. Sams from across the street left, and Honor breathed a sigh of relief. I hugged her. "Honor Maddox, you were a hit! They loved your artwork! They love you! I tell you, I haven't had this much fun since poodle skirts were in style and Marty Claypoole was reachin' up under mine."

'Course, Honor didn't let herself enjoy it much. No, she just flipped on back to her sorry self.

"You think she only bought that painting because she knows me?"

"'Course not," I said.

"Well, where's he going to put a painting of a shell?"

"Anywhere he pleases."

"They hated that mermaid's purse, I could tell. Why in the world did they buy it?"

"Oh, stop it, Honor," I said. "Leave yourself alone. They liked your work. Your paintin's are goin' into people's homes, into their lives. There are little pieces of you floatin' all over this island now. Little pieces scattered about, like seeds."

She'd planted seeds that day, Honor had. I was so proud. Alice would have been proud too. And she would have called her that night had she not been so tired. By the time the last guests had gone home, though, Honor had crawled up the stairs and fallen into bed with no dinner and no bath. Just head first.

I had to come in after the poor thing was asleep and take her borrowed shoes off.

23

Waccamaw Memorial Hospital,
Murrells Inlet
December 14, 2006

Alice

As death approaches, hearing is often the last sense to leave. Assume every word you say can be heard and understood, even if the dying person is unresponsive.

Wayne had a fit, but I've refused to go home. I brought my overnight bag and that's just what I intend to do—stay overnight at the hospital.

I lie on the cot they bring in for me and recount every word I said to Honor while she was awake. I read more of her notes.

I'm clinging to them now. They make me feel like I was with her on St. Anne's—or that her spirit is still here in this room though her body doesn't show it. Her words help me feel connected, and I'm so thankful she's written them.

I finally fall asleep.

At daylight, the first thing I hear makes my heart nearly stop. A low grumble is coming from Honor's throat. I jump to sitting and swing my leg down gently to the floor. "Honor?"

I push to standing and go to her side, sitting next to her and rubbing her hands. "I'm here, Honor. It's me, Alice."

"Mmmm." She makes a noise, and I know she can hear me.

"Are you waking up, sweetie? You feel like you want to wake up?" My excitement gets away with me, and I go to the window and pull back the curtain, flooding the room with light. "Oh look, Honor. The sun's coming up. What a beautiful sunrise. Can you see these colors?"

I wait patiently for Honor to open her eyes and nearly cheer when she does. What happens next is one of those things that will haunt me until my dying day.

Honor's eyes open slowly, as if she's trying to remember how to use her eyelids. She turns her head slightly toward me and the window and stares.

"It's . . . upside down," she says, fretting.

"What?"

"Everything's upside down!"

I'm panicking. I don't know what to do. I pull the curtains

shut and move close to her, holding her head in my chest and rocking slightly. "Shhh, shhh. It's okay. I'm sorry. I'm so sorry. Just close your eyes." I reach over her and grab the nurse call button. "Can I get someone in here, please?!"

The morning nurse comes in and looks at me inquisitively. "Everything all right?" She walks to Honor and grabs her wrist, feeling for a pulse. Honor is now lying back, her eyes closed again. I can't tell if she's awake or not so I take the nurse into the hallway.

"She's seeing upside down!" I tell her. "What's wrong? I've never heard of that!"

"Let me see if a doctor can talk to you."

"Are you serious? Can't you just tell me? That's not normal. Is she getting worse? She's getting worse, isn't she?!"

"I'll send the doctor in to see you, okay? Just a few minutes." She touches my arm and then walks back to the nurses' station and picks up the telephone. I wait there in the hall until I see Dr. So-and-so.

"Good morning," he says, picking Honor's chart off the back of the door. "I understand she's having vision problems today."

"She's seeing upside down!"

"Mm hmm. This happens sometimes when there's a tumor in the brain. We tried radiation to reduce the swelling, but I'm afraid it's putting pressure on her optical nerves."

"So there's nothing we can do?"

"I'm afraid not."

I don't know what to say.

The doctor touches my elbow before walking away. It seems everyone in this hospital is touching me now, as if it's the only thing they can do. I don't want to be touched. It's a bad sign—this touching.

I peek back in on Honor. She's peaceful again. So I grab my purse and crutches and wander out to find some coffee. I need to refresh. I sense the mountain in front of me getting steeper, and I need all the lift I can muster.

I drink my coffee in the cafeteria and grab a bagel and bring it back up with me. Out in the hallway I prepare myself to enter the room again. I pray for strength. I pray for a miracle. I breathe in deeply, let it out, and then push on the door.

I could just die when I see who's sitting there on the edge of Honor's bed.

"Hey, Alice," he says, standing. Brett! Honor's ex-boyfriend is here! The one she worked so hard to get away from. The one who took her money, took her dignity! Brett is *here.*

He walks over to me and hugs me tight. I think I might scream.

"What are you doing here?" I ask him, incredulous.

"I came just as soon as I found out," he tells me. "Wow, I can't believe it. She's so young. 'Course, I always thought she had the body type that could develop cancer. She really should have taken better care of herself."

I want to throttle him. "Brett, what are you doing here? You don't need to be here."

"Are you kidding? Of course I came. As soon as Wayne told me how sick she was—"

"What? Wayne called you?" I go to cover my mouth. I look over at Honor and see she's still sleeping, but I've read the pamphlet on dying. I know she might be able to hear us, so I grab his fat arm and haul him out the door.

"You need to leave. Honor doesn't want you here. It's over, Brett."

"Gee thanks. I know it's over, Alice, but I loved her. I still love her. She's *dying* in there." He says "dying" like it's a communicable disease.

"She might wake up again. And trust me, she will not be happy to see you."

"How do you know?" he says, getting agitated. "I drove all the way up here to see her. I have some things I'd like to say to her. You're not the only one who loves her, you know." I can't believe his gall. I want so much to punch his lights out. "Besides," he adds, "your kids are home. You should be spending some time with them too. It's the holidays."

"What? Is that why he called you? It is! It *is* why he called you, so that I would come back home! Of all the—"

Just then the heart monitor in Honor's room starts beeping. I hobble past Brett, and he follows me. Two nurses slide in after us and tend to her.

"Is she okay? Help her! Is she all right?" I look at Brett like, *See what you did? I'm going to kill you for killing her!*

"Her monitor just came off," a nurse says. "She's all right. Must have slipped off her finger somehow."

I go to Honor's side and rub her forehead. I lean in and kiss her softly on the cheek. I wonder, *Did she take the monitor off herself?*

When the nurses finally leave, Brett and I sit there in thick silence, staring at Honor.

"You're not family," I whisper.

"I'm her common-law husband," he whispers back. "I am *too* family."

"She hasn't lived with you in almost a year, Brett. You are not her family."

"I'm not leaving," he says. And I see my spirit leap from my body, jump across Honor's bed, and strangle him.

"I'm not leaving either." He looks at me with a cocky smile. I'm ready for a fight.

"Why are you here, Brett?" I plead. He says nothing, so I threaten him. "You better not upset her. So help me . . . you better not upset my sister."

I pull out my bagel and move to the chair by the window. Then I bring out Honor's notes and begin reading. It's hard to get, though, because every other minute I'm either fuming that Brett is in the room with us or furious that Wayne called him. I can't believe Wayne stooped so low. I mean, I know he doesn't care much for my sister, but this? After what Wayne pulled, I'll be hog-tied and bound before I go back home while Honor is in here. My girls will just have to come visit with me at the hospital, and that is all there is to it.

24

Alice

As swallowing becomes difficult and the appetite subsides, the dying person may lose interest in food and drink. This is a normal part of the dying process.

My sweet girls make my favorite breakfast the next morning and bring it from home—French toast with powdered sugar, syrup, and fresh fruit, even a thermos of hot coffee. I'm grateful for the break from hospital food, even though eating is the last thing on my mind, and thankful to see a couple of loving faces.

Brett is snoring on the cot when they get here. I slept in a chair all night with my foot propped up, and I'm dying to stand up and stretch. We stand quietly looking at Honor. She isn't awake, but I can tell the difference a day has made. Her face seems more withdrawn and her skin even more pale. Is it possible she's declining so quickly? I grab a wet cloth and gently wash her cheeks, nose, chin, and forehead. Through it all, she doesn't stir. The girls remain deathly still.

"Let's go out into the waiting room," I whisper, pointing to Brett.

"What is he doing here?" Melody asks when we're safely out of earshot.

"If I only knew," I tell her.

"How did he know she was here? I didn't think she even talked to him anymore."

"As far as I know, she doesn't." The girls look at me, confused. "Apparently your father called him."

"What?" Melody asks. "Why would he do that?"

"Not sure," I say, trying hard not to bad-mouth Wayne. He is their father after all.

"Dad just had to mess things up," says Sarah, becoming heated. I keep my mouth shut. Out of the two, Sarah is the most distrustful of others. The sad thing is, she usually gets people just about right.

"I'm sure he just did what he thought was best," I say, ending the subject. "Now pour me some of that coffee, please. And is that French toast! My goodness, y'all are wonderful. My angels. You just don't know how ready I am for a home-cooked meal."

We sit silently while the girls eat their French toast. I sip my coffee and nibble on some fruit, but the sight of food is making me ill. Each of us is thinking about Honor. None of us knows what to say. Finally, Sarah pipes up. "So what do the doctors say?"

"Say? Not much. They say there's nothing they can do."

"So what then? You just sit here and wait till she . . . Mom, I just don't get it. How could Honor not know she was this sick?"

"I don't know. I think . . . maybe she did know," I tell her.

"Well, did *you*?"

"No." Sarah and I stare at each other, and she knows I'm telling the truth.

"Why would she not tell you she has cancer? You're like her closest friend. Y'all are sisters!"

"I don't know, sweetie. I've been racking my brain trying to figure it out. But whatever her reasons . . . well, it's too late for that now."

Agitated, Sarah stands up and throws her food away. "I can't eat. Let's just go back in."

"Listen," I say, putting my hand up to stop her. "Honor probably won't wake up, but if she does, I do not want her getting upset, all right? It's important that we be as supportive as possible right now."

"We know, Mom," says Melody. "Don't worry. She's our aunt too. She's like . . . we love her just as much as you do."

We pad down the hallway, and I use my crutch to hold the door open for the girls. Inside the room, the cot is empty, and I'm praying Brett has finally gone home.

When I see him sitting on the bed next to Honor, my body stiffens. There's a clipboard on her stomach, and he's attempting to wrap her fingers around a pen. Honor's eyes are open and as big around as she can get them.

"What is going on?" I demand. Brett looks like I've caught him with his pants down.

"I just need her to sign one little thing for me. It's nothing really."

"You what? Let me see this!" I grab the clipboard and read the paper on it. "You're trying to get her to sign away property? Are you kidding me, Brett? In all my life I cannot imagine a more selfish thing to do! Look at her, you—disgusting man! Look at her! Oh hey, honey . . ." I lean down, hovering over her, trying desperately to protect her. "I'm so sorry he's here," I whisper, kissing her on her forehead.

"Give it . . . to me," she says weakly.

"But—"

Honor is shaking her head. "Alice. I'll sign."

"No, Honor, you can't!"

"Please," she says with great effort.

I hate him.

I don't say anything more. Brett hands her the pen and guides her hand to the red *X*. I watch in horror as Honor signs her life away. *That leech!* I can't believe he actually came up here for that. He's a worm, a low-life, not worthy of Honor. What did she ever see in him? The user. Now Honor truly has nothing. He's stripped her bare of everything now.

"Go," I tell him with the ferocity of a lioness. "You got what you came for. Now leave my sister alone."

Sarah opens the door and stands there waiting for him, so Brett grabs his jacket. He pauses and looks over at Honor, but she turns her head. She wants nothing to do with him. Brett seems to be considering words but then walks out without saying goodbye.

After he's gone, the girls and I huddle around Honor. "I'm so sorry I left you here with him!" I tell her. "I had no idea he was going to do that. I'm so sorry!"

"Don't," she whispers. "Let him have it." After she swallows, she adds, "I have what I need right here." Honor attempts a smile and looks at me with angel eyes, then at Sarah and Melody. I put my head down on her stomach and hold her, crying softly. Then Melody rests her head on Honor's blanket-covered legs, and Sarah does the same. We hold on to one another, and time stands still. I wish with all my heart that it could simply stop right here with the heat of everyone I love burning into me. Life-breath moves through us all, binding us. The moment permanently etches into my soul.

Miraculously, Honor stays awake for a little while. She asks the girls how they're doing in school. She asks about boys. She tries to smile a couple times when they go on about normal-life things. And none of us mention dying or death. It's there though, like a fifth guest. Death is between us, all around us.

Waiting.

Honor is resting. That's what I say to myself. In my head, I say over and over, *Honor is resting. She's just resting. She's resting nicely. Honor is resting.*

I'm going crazy.

I want Honor to wake up. I want the green tinge to wash off of her skin. I want someone to take all of the tubes and wires and beeping things out of her room, away from her. I want to kidnap Honor, throw her over my shoulder, and walk to Mecca. I would walk to the ends of the earth to save her. I would walk until my feet bled for her face to fill up with life again. I want my old Honor back. I'm the older child. I'm supposed to go first. That was our unspoken deal, wasn't it? The older child gets to go first. It's unnatural for me to be watching my baby sister die.

Oh, dear God. She's dying! Please don't let her die!

In her written words, I can see Honor is learning so much on St. Anne's. Is she still there on St. Anne's? This body here doesn't look like Honor.

I'm having a very hard time staying in touch with reality.

I turn my focus to Brett. And Wayne. Anger nips at me, a mangy dog. I am trapped. Anger. Fear. Self-pity. Who am I without Honor in this world? I do not have a world without Honor. If she dies, will she cease to exist?

Will *I* cease to exist?

25

St. Anne's Isle
September 18, 2006

Honor

The morning after the art showing, I stayed in bed until ten o'clock. When I finally rolled downstairs, I saw Duchess, naked again, sunning out on the back deck. Oh good heavens. Is she depressed again? Just when I was starting to feel better. I thought we were doing so well. She'd been wearing clothes so often, so naturally. I figured we were safely past the nudity phase.

I knocked on the sliding glass door before walking out, shielding my eyes from the sun and her bare parts.

"Mornin', sunshine!" she called in a very chipper voice.

"You sound like you're feeling good," I told her. "Why the no-clothes look?"

"Tan lines, Honor. Don't like 'em. Ain't gonna have 'em. You ever seen me with a tan line?"

"Uh-uh."

"Well, you never will, neither. How you feelin' today? You been in bed so long, I was 'bout to call Mr. Cutie Pie Officer to haul you on out of your bedroom."

"Funny," I said, walking to the rail, careful not to lean on it but lapping up the fresh air.

"Yesterday sure was somethin', wasn't it?" she said. "My, my, my. I can't remember havin' such a good time at a party and still bein' sober. And everybody loved your work. I wouldn't be a bit surprised if you don't get asked to go in the Pelican Gallery. You're every bit as good as those folks, you know."

I smiled, thinking back on the pride I'd felt whenever one of my canvases walked out the door.

"Let's celebrate your success by goin' swimmin'," Duchess declared, rolling over to sit up. I watched as her spare tire fully inflated.

"Oh, I don't have a suit," I told her sheepishly. I'd never gotten my things out of my stowaway car, and I was suddenly embarrassed about it. It really was time I called a locksmith and got my life together. I could afford a locksmith now.

"Don't need a suit," she said.

"What? Oh no. Um, no thanks."

"Oh, come on, Honor. No one's gonna see us down there. Not a soul around. And if they do see us, what's the harm in that? You're an attractive young woman. And I'm a . . . well . . . a woman anyway."

"Skinny-dipping, Anne? In the middle of the day?" I started laughing.

"Have I steered you wrong yet, Miss Honor? You didn't want to show off your paintin's, now did you? That went pretty well, I'd say. Come on. You don't know the word *freedom* till you've gone skinny-dippin' in the Atlantic before noon. Trust me on this."

Don't ask what got into me. Don't ask me why I didn't go running in the other direction. Somehow, I thought the newness of it—of doing something this outrageous—might work better than coffee to get my blood pumping. I was still hopelessly sluggish and achy, as if a fever wasn't too far off in my future.

"Let's go," I told her, eyes wide, daring her, daring myself to feel better. She hopped up and ran for the stairs. "Last one in's a rotten egg!"

Duchess flopped her fanny down one stair at a time and out through the sand dunes. I pounced after her, feeling invigorated and strangely out-of-body. She was already neck deep when I reached the edge of the water.

I stuck my toe in and felt the coolness of it. I turned around to see if anyone was on the beach. No one was. The air was warm and I inhaled deeply, closing my eyes. *This is crazy,* I told myself. Then I stepped out of my shorts and threw them back a couple feet so they wouldn't get wet. I lifted my shirt up and peeled it over my head in a flash, my eyes on the horizon.

I started wading into the water, a huge grin on my face. It did feel liberating. In my whole adult life I'd never done this—never allowed myself this simple little childish freedom.

Duchess was splashing around and cat-calling. I pushed closer and closer, laughing as my legs struggled against the breaking waves. I felt wonderful. Forget all those aches and pains. *Maybe this is it,* I thought. Maybe this was the cleansing I'd needed all along. I was baptizing myself in the elixir of life.

I loved how the cold water tickled my waist, and I turned my head to the sky. *I want to live,* I thought. "I want to live!" I screamed, believing it truly for the first time. I fell back into the water. My head went under, and I heard the rush of water stream in my ears, then silence. I stayed underwater for at least a minute, feeling life press in all around me.

When I finally pushed off the sandy bottom and stuck my neck out, I looked around and found Duchess. "This is incredible!" I told her. But the look on her face stopped my heart. Duchess wasn't laughing anymore. She wasn't even smiling. In fact, I'd never seen this serious look on her face before.

Duchess

"What's wrong?" Honor asked me. "You all right?" She treaded closer.

I couldn't speak.

"Talk to me. Are you okay? Did something sting you?" She came closer still.

"Honor," I said, trying hard to find my voice. Her brown hair was slick and her head floated on top of the water as if she had no body. "Honor, honey, stand up a second."

"What? Why?"

"Just do it."

Her face crinkled up, confused, and I could tell she'd become self-conscious all of a sudden about being naked. "No, it's too cold," she told me.

"Honor, there's somethin' wrong. Please stand up. Look at your chest, honey."

"Huh?" Honor stood up then and looked down. In a million years, I'll never forget what I saw.

Her right breast was covered in goose bumps, but otherwise normal. The left one was not. It was almost twice as big and mis-shapen like a day-old balloon, loosing its air.

Honor reached up and cradled the bottom of it, and I put my hand to my mouth, horrified.

"Oh my goodness," she muttered.

Oh, dear God, no.

Honor swore she'd had no idea. But how could she not have known? How could the swelling have come on so suddenly?

"Think back, Honor. Have you been looking in the mirror?"

"Well, not especially. But last night I wore that dress of yours. It fit me perfectly. No problems. No enlarged parts."

But this morning, her left breast was swollen. Disfigured. Horrifying. I just couldn't make sense of it.

"Well, I have had some bug bites on that breast for about a week now," Honor said, "but nothing more."

"Bug bites?"

"Yes. I must have gotten bitten by something." Honor was drying off now in the house.

"Honor, sweetie, you need to go see a doctor."

"You think?"

"*Yes.* Go put some clothes on," I said. "I'll pull the car out."

"But we have to go all the way to town for that. Let's just wait a day," she said. "Let's see if the swelling goes down."

"Honor, no."

"Anne. Please. Just give it a day, all right? I know I got bitten by something. It's probably from that room under the house where your paints are. There are tons of spiderwebs in there."

I looked at her, wary. I guess she could be right . . .

"How about just getting me some aspirin and an ice pack," she said. "And coffee. Let's see how that does me." She smiled at me, but I was still real concerned.

"You promise me if it's not better in the mornin' you'll go see a doctor?"

"Yes," she told me.

I had no idea she was lying straight to my face.

Honor

*I didn't want to go to the doctor because I had no insur*ance. With no insurance, I would become more of a burden, financially, emotionally, and otherwise—to Duchess and to you. And what if something truly was wrong? What if I had cancer or a disease equally terrible? Deep down in the pit of my soul, I knew something was truly wrong with me. I must have. I just wouldn't allow the thought to take root in my brain.

And yes, even though I was finally at a fairly good place in my life—at least I knew I wanted to live—there was still a voice inside me, a man's voice, saying, "This, Honor Maddox, is your just deserts."

26

Alice

It's Thursday. It's been four days since the car accident. Four days since I learned Honor was dying. Four days since I learned that I don't know who I am anymore. I thought I had it all together. My life was perched precariously yet firmly on the edge of a cliff. Now the ground beneath me is crumbling.

"Can you bring me something for a headache?" I ask the attending nurse.

She looks at me cautiously. "Well, we're not really supposed to dispense anything unless you're a patient."

"I *am* a patient. See my foot? Please," I beg. Surely she can see I need it.

"I'll see what I can do," she says and walks away on padded shoes.

I watch Honor's breathing becoming more labored, and I think my head is going to explode. I need something to kill this pain. If I had a bottle of wine here I'd turn it up and guzzle it in a heartbeat. I've never been drunk before in my life. Been tipsy a few times but never drunk. I've seen what it can do to a person. Wayne is a drunk. Oh, he pulls himself together by morning and goes to work and gets his job done, but I know the truth. I can tell a difference in him when he's had just one beer.

Just off Murrells Inlet there's a place called Drunken Jack Island. Growing up, we'd hear the legend of a pirate who'd been left there accidentally with no provisions except cases and cases of rum. Months later when his shipmates returned for the cargo, all they found were empty rum bottles and the bleached white bones of a pirate. At this moment, I'd give anything to be Drunken Jack, to be able to drink my problems away. I feel like Honor and I have been stranded here. Alone. Hopeless. Our bones bleaching white.

I lean over and lay my head on Honor's pillow. "We're in this together," I tell her. "We're in this together."

I've always been the good sister. I never got into any trouble. Never even thought I was capable of it. Mother and Daddy never really had to have a firm word with me because I listened to them. Unlike Honor, I never fought against their authority. I kept a smooth ride of things, not bucking the system. Never fighting back.

I feel differently now, as if some wild animal has crawled into my skin while I was sleeping on that hard cot. I am a raging bull. I'm raring for a fight. But there is no fight to be had. I am furious the doctors can't do anything more, yet I know they've done and are doing everything they possibly can. I want them to do more! I don't *want* them to go home to their families on Christmas Eve in a few days. I want them to stay here with me and suffer, and make her well.

Why do all the good die young? It's true, isn't it? I suppose that confirms I'm not as good as I've always pretended to be.

Honor

Alice. I'm taking you back to the summer of 1971. You were thirteen. I was eleven. You had a crush on that boy, Charles? James? I can't remember, but you were all goo-goo over him. To me, you chattered constantly about his eyes, how good he was at baseball, how different he was from all the others, but you were vigilant to stay quiet around Mother and Daddy. I think that may be what did it—your silence. Whenever Mother asked you about boys, you clammed up, face white. She knew you were getting interested in them.

I really couldn't care less about boys. They were silly, slimy, foul-mouthed beasts who knocked me off the swings and called me names. That summer I had begun menstruating early. My chest was two marbles, poking out for the entire world to see. I hated my chest. The boys called me Skeeter Bites. I hated them too.

That was the summer Mother and Daddy had befriended Preacher Bullard and his wife. I'm not sure why Mother felt it necessary to bring them into our lives. I was just fine with only seeing them in church on Sundays, every other one or so that I attended anyway. I remember Mrs. Bullard would sit straight as a rocket fingering her organ. I hated organ music, and I would yawn during the preacher's messages. Mother would reach down and pinch the skin underneath my leg until tears rolled down my cheeks. Then I'd straighten up on the pew and "behave" like she wanted me to.

Daddy and the preacher had discovered they shared a love for boats. Daddy had a plain old runabout and Preacher Bullard had a brand new sport cruiser. It was the first time, really, that Daddy had an adult friend to do anything with. A man of God was a suitable playmate for him according to Mother, and Mrs. Bullard was perfect for sewing and quilting, sharing recipes and gossiping about the ills of the community. All in all the relationship seemed to be working out well.

You and I were required to call the preacher "sir" and Mrs. Bullard "ma'am" like we would anyone else, but we were also expected to behave even better when they were around. We were the fruits of Mother's womb. She strove for perfection, and we needed to be as close to it as possible in front of them.

We were sitting at supper one Friday night with the Bullards across from us. Daddy was at one end of our polished dining room table and Mother was at the other. They were sharing niceties, the four of them, and you and I were minding our p's and q's, slathering butter on our cornbread, when Preacher Bullard asked a question.

"Alice, are you and your friends gettin' interested in boys yet?" We looked up at him in horror. "Why, I can remember when my Rebecca was your age, we had to have the talk with her. You know, the s-e-x talk."

Mrs. Bullard glared at him. "Rebecca was from his previous marriage," she explained. "His wife—God rest her soul—she passed away, you know."

The preacher seemed unfazed and persisted. "Well, are you, Alice? Interested in boys, that is?"

"N-no, sir," you said, your face deflating. I wanted to cover it up with my napkin and save you.

I looked up at Mother and her mouth had dropped open. Then I looked at Daddy. His cheeks were stuffed full, and he stared intently at his Crowder peas.

Mother found her voice. "Do you really think it's time for that? I—it's awfully young, don't you think?"

"Oh, Marie. Let's not be naïve," he scolded. "Times are a-changin'. Evil waits for no age."

Well, that shut Mother up. In fact, it shut everyone up. You and I ate faster than the speed of light then. We cleaned our plates and practically licked them so we could ask to be excused.

When Daddy told us it was all right, we ran back to our room to play with Barbie dolls. We'd escaped. But I remembered the look on Mother's face when we left the table. I could tell she was thinking, hard.

The next day was a Saturday. I woke up and opened my eyes in the dim light to see Mother jostling you, whispering. Whatever Mother wanted this early in the morning, I certainly didn't want any part of it. I watched as you pulled some shorts on and then I turned over, closed my eyes again, and fell back to sleep.

You were gone all day and I was bored. I'd asked Daddy where you went, and he told me you were out on the boat with Preacher Bullard. My heart sank. I remembered the look on your face at dinner. Mother must have seen it too. Now she'd sicced the preacher on you. I made up my mind then to be as good and invisible as possible to avoid the same fate.

Just before suppertime, you walked in with the preacher right behind you. He had his hand on your shoulder and was telling something to Mother and Daddy which pleased them to no end. You looked like you wanted to crawl in a hole. You were green, and when I asked you what the preacher had talked about, you told me, "Shut up, Honor." You'd never said that to me. It hurt me. I knew it must have been awful, whatever it was.

I left you in the bedroom, and when it was time for supper and you didn't come out, Mother and Daddy conferred and actually let you skip a meal, remember? That was a first. Whatever business you'd had with the preacher, it was terrible for you and mighty important to Mother and Daddy.

Well, my plan of being invisible and good didn't last very long. The following Saturday, Mother woke me up when it was still dark outside. You were asleep. "Preacher Bullard wants to take you fishing, Honor," she whispered, smiling like it was my birthday and she was so proud. My heart stopped then. I knew you hadn't been the same since you'd gone fishing with him the week before.

My red and white bobber was sitting on top of the water, and I eyed it hard, waiting for it to submerge. *Come on fishy, fishy. Give me a nibble.* I'd always loved fishing. I loved the thrill of watching that bobber go up and down and knowing that if I jerked it at precisely the right moment, that fish would be hooked and mine. What I didn't like was the taking-the-fish-off-the-hook part.

"Let me help you with that," said Preacher Bullard, grinning his square teeth at me. "You're quite a fisherman. Or fisher-woman, as it were."

No one had ever called me a woman before.

He grabbed the croaker carefully and wrenched the hook out of its mouth. "Ooowee! Wait till your daddy sees what a good girl you are." I grinned on the inside. Being a good girl for Daddy meant everything to me.

I couldn't stand watching it. The fish gaped at me, staring. "It's too small," I told him, feeling guilty all of a sudden. "Let's throw him back."

"You sure?" he asked.

"Yes, sir."

"Well, all right then." He set the fish gently on top of the water and let it swim away. Then he stuck both hands in the water and washed, drying them on his pants leg.

After adding a squirming bloodworm to my hook, I cast my rod back in the water, thinking that this wasn't so bad after all. I started thinking about you, Alice, wondering why you were being such a big baby about going fishing with the preacher. He wasn't so bad. He was just old and stodgy like Granddaddy.

"You want a Coke-cola?" he asked me. I was shocked. His hand was outstretched, holding a full bottle. You and I always had to split one, and we only got one about once in a blue moon on special occasions. Here he was, offering me a full one, all to myself. A flicker of fear shot through me, wondering what Mother would do if she knew I was drinking soda all willy-nilly on a regular ole day.

"Thank you," I said. Just to spite her I took it from him. I put

the cold bottle up to my lips and felt the bubbles tickle my nose.
I let a sip roll down my tongue and closed my eyes, savoring every
sugary drop. *This is heaven,* I thought. *And if Mother gets angry,
I'll just tell her the preacher gave it to me. She can't argue with that.*

Preacher Bullard reeled in a nice-sized whiting, and I hooted
and hollered for him while it dangled in the air. When he had
thrown it in the cooler, he washed his hands again and things
settled down. I was sipping my Coke and watching a pelican dive
into the water when he said to me, "Miss Honor? Mrs. Bullard
and I have become quite fond of your mama and daddy. They're
good people."

"Yes, sir," I said.

"And now, they love you and Alice to pieces. Did you know
that?"

"Yes, sir."

"Well now, your mama and daddy have asked me, as pastor
of the Goodwill Baptist Church, as a good friend of the family,
and as a man of God who knows right from wrong, to talk with
you about something very important."

My heart stilled.

"What they'd like me to talk to you about is *sex*. You ever
heard of sex, Miss Honor?"

My brain started bubbling over. My heart was racing so fast,
I grabbed it to make sure I wasn't going to pass out. The next few
minutes seemed like an eternity. Preacher Bullard told me boys
were going to be interested in me soon, if they weren't already.

He said that nothing good could be found in a young boy's head. It was just pure evil. What he said was that it was my job to recognize that evil and bring the fear of God back into these boys if they tried something on me.

"You know what they might do?" he asked.

I couldn't speak.

"They might try this." Preacher put his arm around my shoulder.

"Seems innocent enough, don't it?"

I nodded, dying, feeling his heat.

"But then look how quickly it can turn into this." Preacher stuck his hand down the front of my shirt and touched my tiny breasts. I froze. I was paralyzed. But he took it as a sign of approval and pressed on. In a flash, Preacher's hand had found its way inside my shorts. I left my body, I think, at that point.

The next thing I knew, I was on my feet, soda bottle clenched in my hand. I'm not sure if I did it on purpose or involuntarily, but the bottle connected with the preacher's jaw. He lunged for me then like the devil himself with fire in his eyes, and I screamed and ducked. Preacher went over the side of the boat headfirst.

I remember hearing a thud and seeing air bubbles come up like popcorn to the surface. I stared into the black water, fixed, wondering what I was going to do when he came back up. I wanted so desperately to go home. To leave this nightmare. I watched the water. Nothing. Nothing. Preacher's feet, still in his boat shoes, finally rose to the air.

I didn't want to help him. There was nothing in me, not the first impulse to jump in after him, to save his life. The truth is, I was glad he was dead. I hoped he was dead. Because at eleven years old, I was now dead. The preacher'd done that to me.

27

Alice

I must have dozed off. Something jolts me awake and I open my eyes, realizing that someone is knocking on the door. I look over at Honor. She's still there, thank God.

A small-framed man walks in. He has a thin bird nose, his hair is thick salt and pepper, and he wears round glasses reminiscent of Radar on *M.A.S.H.*

I move to sitting and realize Honor's papers have been left open on my lap for anyone to see. I carefully fold and scoot them under my seat for safekeeping.

"Hello," he says. "I'm Fred, the chaplain here. There is no religion listed on Ms. Maddox's chart, so I'm just here to see if I might be of some service to you."

A chaplain. A preacher man.

"Uh, no, thank you. I—"

"Are you the sister?"

"Yes."

"Is your sister a religious person?"

"No."

"I understand how difficult a time like this can be for loved ones. You may have many questions about—"

"I'm sorry, Chaplain," I say, turning brusque. "This really is not a good time."

"Oh," he says, looking only slightly uncomfortable. Then as if he'd been expecting me to say these exact words, he nods and smiles.

"I understand, Miss . . ."

"Chandler. Alice."

"Miss Alice. I pray that you will be comforted in this most difficult time. If you would like to talk, day or night, we have a small chapel on the—"

"That won't be necessary," I tell him, ruffled. "Thank you though."

He nods and turns around, opens the door, and walks out. I realize I have been practically holding my breath the whole time he was in the room. I am aware that I am utterly unglued in the presence of a so-called man of God. This one, I'm sure, is harmless, but I certainly don't want him anywhere near Honor and me right now. He is everything that has gone wrong—in the flesh.

Honor

What must you think of me, Alice? I hope you still love me. I don't blame you if you don't. But I have to go on. I've come this far.

I left Preacher Bullard in the water and threw his rod overboard. I started his boat and brought it back to our dock, blood pounding in my ears. I was crying by then, and the tears helped to convey that I'd had nothing to do with the preacher's death. In fact, I wasn't even suspected. I told Mother and Daddy my first big lie, that he'd fallen in while reeling a big fish. That he'd hit his head on the shallow bottom. Part of that was true. And if I thought it long enough, I might believe it too. Yes, I became a good liar that day in 1971 and never looked back.

That evening, Alice, you and I exchanged a look before going to bed. We never spoke anything about the preacher, but I knew he'd done the same thing to you. I understood what was wrong with you. How far had he gone? I could only imagine, but I figured it was further than he'd made it with me. And knowing he'd hurt you just fueled my sense of justice. I was glad he was gone for good.

Did you wonder if he'd had his sex talk with me too? Did you talk yourself into thinking it probably didn't happen? That he'd died before laying a hand on me? Was that your justification for never saying a word? Never asking me a thing? I'm not angry with you, of course I'm not. But it would have been nice to share this with you years ago. I didn't want to burden you, and I'm sure you felt the same and didn't want to burden me either.

You and I never talked about that summer. We never spoke about the preacher dying or Mother mourning. Life changed after that. For everyone. Mother and Daddy never made close friends again after Mrs. Bullard moved away. And I was now a murderer, not to anyone else, but to me and to God. We both knew the truth. And I grew a crust around me, impenetrable even to you.

Forgive me, Alice. *Forgive me, God.*

I can still hear his voice, the preacher's, and he tells me things, you know. To this day. He says I'm going to hell. That I deserved being barren, childless. "Don't mess with the preacher man," he tells me. "Don't mess with a man of God."

Because of what happened that summer, I've had as little to do with God and religion and supposed "people of faith" as humanly possible. But in my last couple months on St. Anne's Isle, He, meaning God, seemed to be everywhere I turned.

I'd lied to Duchess. I told her the swelling had gone down in my left breast. It hadn't. It had gotten worse. And the right breast was looking strange too. My skin was red and itchy and looked like the peel of an orange. I felt for lumps. But of course I had lumps. I'd always had lumps—*fibrous tissue* is what one doctor had called it. *Fibrocystic breasts* is what another had said. It was nothing to worry about, they'd told me.

I continued painting and went on with life. I kept all feelings of fear, of what was happening to my body, completely at bay. Totally out of reach. No one from the Pelican Gallery had asked me to put my work in there, but I painted anyway. Islanders started asking me to paint their furniture. I needed the money, and I was flattered. So I painted a lampshade with seagulls on it for a little girl's room. I painted a marsh scene on a chest of drawers. And I was painting cozy chair scenes on a buffet table for an old lady—a reading nook, beach chairs, a rocking chair on a porch—when you called.

"Honor, honey, it's your sister," Duchess said when she handed me the phone. She covered the receiver and whispered, "Why does she always ask me how I'm feelin'? What does she think I am, old? An invalid?"

I took the phone from her.

"Hey, Alice." I waved Duchess away like, *I have it now, thank you,* and she sulked out. "I swear she'll be leaving here soon, but poor thing just can't seem to get it together."

"Well, maybe she can come with you then. What are your plans for the holidays? Are you coming up here?"

"The holidays! My goodness, is it almost that time already? Well, I guess I'll come up there. But don't worry about my roommate. I think she's going to see her kids. Are your girls coming home?" You told me they were, but I was cringing for so many reasons. Yes, I wanted desperately to see you and the girls. But once again, another year had come where I was broke and wondered how in the world I was going to buy Christmas presents. I decided with you on the line that I'd paint presents for you all. *Voilá*. It was done.

We planned on having me drive up on December 16, more than a week before Christmas. "You sure Mr. Man doesn't mind my coming?" I asked.

"Wayne? Of course not. It wouldn't be Christmas without you here."

Christmas. That's when it hit me. I was going to see you in less than two months and at the moment I was in no shape for it. It was time to face facts. My health was declining quickly. It was time to do something. My doing nothing approach seemed to be doing more harm than good.

I decided it was time to find Blondell. I'd avoided it as long as I could, but I'd avoided going to the doctor too. At this point, Blondell seemed a whole lot cheaper. And I realized on some level I was in deep trouble.

It had come on fairly quickly. I was extremely ill and thin in those days. I was vomiting quite a bit, but I'd taken to doing it in the privacy of my bathroom, away from Duchess' eyes and ears, like some teenaged bulimic hiding her secret. Duchess had been just as chipper as could be and had taken to walking along the beach now that it was cooler and now that I was spending so much time painting. She was keeping her clothes on, and I didn't want to do anything to change that. She was too fragile to have to start worrying about me.

Duchess was on the beach one afternoon, and I knew I could slip away. I lumbered down the front steps and practically crawled to the playground. The cool breeze of October helped me get there, and the nannies seemed thrilled to see me when I arrived. It had been about a month since I'd seen them at my art showing.

"Miss Honor!" squealed Willa. "Look-ee, Miss Honor done come today! How you doin'? Feelin' good? You lookin' skinny. Real skinny. Chile, you been eatin' over there to Duchess' house? She ain't feedin' you?"

"I'm just fine," I told her and said my hellos to everyone. "Is Miss Blondell coming today?"

"Blondell? No, she don't come much no more. Ever since you took to paintin' and all. She back to the house. Why? You wanna see her?"

"Well, it's been awhile. I miss her. I'd love to see how she's doing."

"Well, go on over then," piped Ruby. "She probably washin' clothes or fixin' supper. She'll be real happy to see you. Want me to run on over with you?"

"Oh no. I know the way."

I said goodbye and that I'd see them all again real soon, I promised. I hoped. Then I tried to walk like a good-feeling person might, upright and steady. By the time I made it to Blondell's front door, I thought I might pass out cold.

There was a thick palmetto tree in front of the house bordered with a ring of conch shells. The mailbox was metal and rusting, and weeds were cropping up around the edge of the porch. Little statues of animals and what appeared to be saints and gnomes lined the overgrown walkway, and there were four white planters filled with herbs on each of four steps leading up to the screened-in porch.

I knocked on the wood frame and then walked right in. At the front door I paused, though, gathering my breath and my nerve. Being there brought back memories of how Blondell had saved my life just months ago. I prayed she might be able to do that for me again.

Blondell looked surprised to see me when she cracked the door open. Not happy, just surprised, more concerned than anything. "On'ry," she said. Then she backed up a step and pulled the door wide, taking in my face, my thin body. I stepped inside and saw Inky the cat staring at me.

"Hey there, Mr. Inky," I said. I tried to reach down and scratch his head but struggled. That's when Blondell knew something was wrong.

"Sit down ya." She grabbed my arms and led me to the couch. The wood floors creaked as we shuffled across them. I smelled vegetables stewing and fought the urge to vomit. "You awrigh'?" she asked. "Don' look good."

"I'm . . . Blondell, I—"

"Spit out, gal. Ya sick?"

My throat caught, and I couldn't speak. Instead, I just nodded and watched the cat. He was lying on the rug now, flicking his tail and eyeing me. I began to tear up.

Blondell sucked in air and made a whistling noise. Then she started praying it seemed, mumbling to herself. She took me by the shoulders and felt my neck, my pulse perhaps. I cried harder and she pulled my head to her frail chest and held it there, very tight. I bawled like a baby then.

By the time the tears had slowed, Blondell was singing and rocking slightly with my hand in hers. I looked up into her dark eyes and said, "I think it's pretty bad." This realization, admitting this to another human being, flooded me with fear. There was urgency all of a sudden. No more time to waste. Maybe Blondell could do something. I knew she was considered a root doctor around these parts. She was a wise Gullah elder with a strong African heritage. She knew how to use what comes from the earth to heal body and spirit. Just about everyone who knew her could attest to that.

"I need to show you something," I said, taking a deep breath, preparing myself to take this leap. There would be no turning back.

Blondell sat up straighter as if firming herself. She nodded her head, so I stood and faced her.

Then I lifted my shirt up.

I wanted to read her face. Blondell remained firm, only her left eye twitched. I knew what she was seeing though, and I wished I could crawl right out of my skin.

"Lawd, chile. Lawd," she said, shaking her head. "Lawd hab mercy pon dis'ya chile."

I lowered my shirt. My fears were confirmed. It was as bad as I thought. I'll never forget what Blondell said to me next. She captured it, the horror, so perfectly—my black skin, hardened and disfigured. I had no more chest. No breasts. Something was ravaging me.

"Da look like de debil eself," she muttered over and over.

The devil himself.

Blondell walked me to the bedroom and put me in her bed, and then she set off to scurrying around the house faster than I'd seen her move. I could hear her footsteps. I just knew she was busy trying to find a remedy for me. I felt like I was home again with Mother fussing over me, preparing my spoon and castor oil. Mother would make me well. I'd come to the right place. Blondell was trying to save me. Why hadn't I come here weeks ago?

I looked over at the stack of Bibles on the chest beside me, and tears ran down my cheeks. I had failed. I'd made yet another terrible decision. At a time when I was ready to start living, I now feared my life might be cut short. My just desert. My just desert.

It was then that I prayed harder than I'd ever done before. *Heal me, God. Please heal me.*

Heal me, God. Heal me!

28

Alice

Heal her, God, please heal her! She's my baby sister. She hasn't had a fair life. This isn't fair. She's so young, God! How could You let this happen? Look how she's suffered! Oh, please!

I bawl and bleat like a lamb on the altar. They say she has only hours, days at most. They've lost all hope. I've lost hope too.

In preparation of Honor's dying, I feel myself retreating from her. I almost want to leave the room, leave the hospital. At times I'm terrified she'll die. At others, I hope she goes quickly and gets it over with. Gets my own death over with. If I could crawl up under the covers beside her and die along with Honor, I think I just might.

Sarah and Melody are here at the hospital and have stepped out of the room for coffee. I know I don't have long.

"Honor. It's me," I whisper, taking her hand in mine. "It's Alice. Honey, I read your letters. I know what happened all those years ago. Honor, you did *not* kill the preacher. Do you hear me? You did not kill him. He was a monster. He abused you. You fought back in self-defense. Honey? Honor, can you hear me?"

I grab her hand and squeeze it, hoping to feel a squeeze back. "Honor, you did not kill the preacher. You've done nothing to be sorry for. You have done nothing to be forgiven for. I just can't believe you've lived your whole life suffering over that. Over him! Honor, I'm glad he died—for what he did to you. For what he did to me. And I'm so sorry I never talked to you about that summer. Please forgive me, Honor. Oh, God, please forgive me!"

Tears are streaming down my face, and I feel the slight pressure of Honor's fingers on mine just as the door swings open. The girls are back. Honor has heard me. She heard me. *Thank you, God.* Honor forgives me.

"Mom?" says Melody. "Mom, is she—"

I shake my head, then lay it down by Honor's side and weep for the little girls who live inside us both.

Honor

Dear Alice,

I am weak. I am unable to use my hand. My nurse, Sadie, is writing.

You would like Blondell. I miss her. She did her best to heal me. You have to know that. She made a poultice from green cockleburs and spread it on my chest. She covered new sores in spiderwebs. She buried lye in the front yard to keep the evil out. She lit candles and prayed. She read the Bible to me. She told me the sickness in my body was a physical manifestation of a spiritual illness. I'd carried poison in my soul for too long. I did not disagree with her. But I continued to believe that if we prayed, if I let her keep treating me and anointing my head with oil, that I might be healed like one of those lepers in the Bible.

I feel just like a leper.

The night I first told her I was ill, Blondell led me in prayer. While lying in her tall bed surrounded by stillness and stale air and a dark-skinned angel, I accepted Jesus as my Lord and Savior, perhaps for the hundredth time. But this time I really meant it. I still don't understand why God chooses not to heal me. I think I have wasted too much time.

Don't waste your time, Alice.

A man came in today to take pictures of my body. It is not a good thing. It means I'm going to be used as an example of what stage four cancer looks like. I will be the poster child for doing nothing. At least they won't show my face. I told them they could take the pictures if they don't show my face.

I feel very strange now. They have started me on morphine. I feel relieved to have told you my secrets. What I want you to understand is that they are your secrets too. They will destroy you if you let them. I have been destroyed.

I am tired.

Dear Alice,

Nurse Sadie is writing for me. She is such a friend.

I don't want to die. I wonder what heaven will be like. I hope Daddy is up there. And Mother too. I don't want to go without you. I don't want to leave you. I'm so sorry.

Blondell told me to go home to you and I refused. I kept thinking there was a chance I might be healed and then you would never have to know about any of this. It was stupid. I know. I have no excuse. I still hope you don't have to see me like this.

At Blondell's house, Duchess was with me around the clock. She begged me to go to the hospital. She cried. She offered to pay for everything. I thought my alternative methods of treatment were working. I was getting blacker and more eaten up every day but fooled myself into believing I was healing. I cannot explain this insanity. There is no way to explain. Blondell told me that airing out my secrets might help, so I lay there for days, confessing every word of my life to her and Duchess. Every bit. And getting it out finally made me realize you needed to hear it too.

I did not plan to come to Murrells Inlet early. The night before, Blondell had rounded up the nannies and the elder men in her community. I could not walk well anymore. They wrapped me in blankets and put me in a wheelbarrow. They wheeled me to a place in the woods by a salt marsh. It was dark except for the full moon. I could smell the pluff mud. I could hear the crickets.

An old black man beat a long stick on the ground once. Then he started singing.

Kneebone bend in the wilderness,
Kneebone bend in the valley

He was singing in prayer, bending down. His body was leaned forward, and he began stomping his feet, small steps at first. Slow at first. Then others joined in the circle. I was in the middle of the circle. Duchess was beside me, holding my hand, crying. Blondell rose to her feet and went out into the circle. She was shuffling her feet. They all were, around and around counterclockwise.

The Gullah people danced. It was a rhythmic jerking motion. Hips, backs, arms, heads. The clapping got louder. The shouting got faster. The songster would call. The people would respond. The circle closed tighter. I closed my eyes. I could feel the rhythm in my painful chest.

By myself. By myself. By myself. By myself.
You know I got to go.
You got to run.

I've got to run.

You got to run.

By myself. By myself. By myself.

I got a letter, I got a letter,

Ol' brownskin.

Tell you what she say.

"Leavin' tomorrow,

Tell you goodbye."

O my Lordy. O my Lordy. O my Lordy. O my Lordy.

Well, well, well. Well, well, well.

I've got a rock.

You got a rock.

Rock is death.

O my Lordy.

O my Lord.

Well, well, well.

Run here, Jeremiah. Run here, Jeremiah.

I must go

On my way. On my way. On my way.

My blood was racing and I knew they were talking to me. Blondell had told me about black spirituals. They were praise songs in the midst of sorrow—they lifted their spirits above the hardships of slavery and healed them. Blondell's parents and grandparents, slaves, had sung spirituals to praise God but also to send coded messages in front of the white men who enslaved them. The songs were an escape to freedom in mind and spirit, and many followed them literally off the plantations to the Underground Railroad. In singing, they were slaves no more.

The morning after the ring shout, I still felt its echoes, and I heeded my call. It was time. I was coming home to see you.

Officer Simmons drove me to Murrells Inlet. He is a wonderful man. Perhaps the only one I've ever met, other than Daddy. I hope you get to meet him. We had stopped in Litchfield Beach. I knew you weren't expecting me, and I was terrified of what you would see. I was trying to freshen up when I collapsed. I woke up at the hospital. And I sent Officer Simmons home the next day even though he wanted to stay.

The doctors told me we could try radiation. I don't know why, but I thought that might be my cure. I was grasping for things, like ropes from heaven. I kick myself for not coming to the hospital earlier. It was so stupid. I am truly ashamed.

I wanted to see progress with my radiation. I wanted to wait to call you until there was hopeful news. The doctors told me to call you. I was insane not to. Still to this day, to this moment, even as I cannot write this letter myself, there is a part of me that believes I am going to live. I'm not going to die. I'm too young. Modern medicine is advanced. I'm in the hospital. They are doing everything possible. I have you to live for. I want to see your girls graduate. I want to dance at their weddings.

I want to watch you find the joy you deserve.

I finally know how to live.

29

Alice

Hallucinations are a normal part of the dying process. Seeing or hearing loved ones who have died is common. This can be unsettling, and you may not know how to respond.

There are no words to describe just how helpless I feel in these last days when death is grabbing hold of Honor and pulling her closer, closer, closer still. I don't have the television on. There are no sounds except the beeping of machinery and muffled footsteps down the hall. My sister has grown so thin that

her chest looks like a barrel, heaving up and down. She is strain-
ing to get air and her breathing has become irregular.

Her morphine has been increased. I ask the doctor, "But isn't
it addictive?"

It's a stupid question. Honor is not leaving this hospital alive.
She will never be addicted to morphine or any other substance. I
have to remind myself of how bad things are on an hourly basis.
My mind is shutting down just like Honor's body. At one point, I
sit in silence as the nurse observes a thick yellow substance trying
to claw its way through her catheter. They're Honor's kidneys, she
says. They're disintegrating. Her body is literally falling apart.

I feel removed from everything, from Honor, from my girls,
from my own soul. I can't touch anything. I've flown off the
earth and am simply going through the motions. My brain has
produced its own sort of morphine. No pain. No pain. No pain.

After four days of sitting at Honor's side, reading her words,
I'm becoming delusional. I cry out to Mother and Daddy. I ask
them to take care of her. I'm pretty sure they answer me back
and say that they will.

Like a sick compulsion, I relive their deaths and grieve all
over again. I imagine the angel of death lurking in the shadows.
He looks something like Brett although taller, leaner. And repeatedly, I beg God to spare Honor's life, although looking at her I
know there can be no miracle now. Too much has been lost.
Honor is barely there anymore. And it's selfish on my part, isn't
it? I need to let her go. She can be with Mother and Daddy again.

She can be with Jesus. Why would I deny her being able to go to heaven? Then it occurs to me. She's leaving me. *She* is going to heaven, and I am staying here.

With Wayne.

Honor

Dear Alice,

Speaking is hard. There are things you need to know now. I am running out of time.

This is what I know:

You are still the thirteen-year-old girl—the one who turned from religion and anything that resembles it. You found the one man on earth who is the opposite of "godly." This felt safe to you. You did this for survival. I know because I did this too.

I know this is true. I have seen your bruises. I know the symptoms. I've known for years. I've done nothing to save you. I don't know how you can ever forgive me. I hope to forgive myself.

It was Thanksgiving. You were pregnant with Melody. I refused him, of course. But I never told you. Or about his affairs. There were many. I thought you might already know, and I didn't want to make your life any harder. It was terrible of me. Please forgive me.

It has taken me a lifetime and now my death to tell you the truth about so many things. Don't let me die for nothing, Alice.

I love you.

30

Alice

I truly don't know if I can stand to look at Wayne again after all he's done, but I don't get the chance to wonder for long. After noon, when the nurse has started her rounds with Honor and then gone on to someone who actually has a chance to live, Wayne shows up with flowers and my favorite feather pillow.

"Hey," he says, sheepishly. He's wearing a leather bomber jacket and blue jeans which hang a little looser these days. He takes a step toward me then stops as if I'm frothing at the mouth and might bite. "I thought you might like this," he says, setting the pillow under my broken foot. Then he puts a small arrangement of winter flowers on the windowsill. "These are from the girls. And me."

If I look at him I know I'll see his hypnotic brown eyes, the sad ones, the ones that always get me to cave. But I can't look at him, let alone speak.

"You gotta believe me, Alice. I had no idea Brett was going to do what he did. I promise you. He seemed really upset when he heard about Honor."

I shake my head, weighing my words.

"Say something, babe. Oh, man. Wow." Wayne backs up a couple steps when he sees Honor. He sits in the chair as far away as he can get from her as if she's contagious. As if death is something *going around*.

It is then that I say it—something that's been brewing inside me for years but lay dormant until this very moment. Something that I suppose I've always known in the foggy depths of my brain, but hadn't confirmed until reading Honor's last letter. I hurriedly shoved it under my rear when Wayne came in, and it's burning like acid beneath me.

"I know what you did." My jaw is tight like a trap. "I know exactly what you did. There's no hiding anymore. You disgust me."

The words, the sound of them coming out of my own prudish mouth, shock me. I close my eyes tight and wish with all I have in me I could just vanish from where I'm sitting, back to a time when all was innocent, when I was completely stupid and ignorant. I understand now how Honor must have felt when she wanted it all to end, and I wish I, too, could just disappear off the face of the earth, never to be seen again.

"Now you listen here," Wayne says, his eyes glowing, fists clenching, his voice a low growl, "I was only trying to help. Don't you ever speak to me that way again! You hear me, Alice? I know you're upset, what with your sister dying and all, but you ever speak to me like that again, and I swear to you, I—"

Sarah clears her throat and Wayne stops in mid-threat. The girls are back in the room now. They always did have good—or bad—timing that way. I flash back to when Sarah was three. She opened the door and saw her daddy holding a gun to my head. That was the first and the last time he ever did that. To this day, Sarah and I have never spoken about it. I have no idea if Sarah remembers. I pray to God that she doesn't.

Wayne stands up and grabs for his keys and says, "I gotta go." Then he leaves me to sit in the stench of decay our marriage has become. It's been dying for such a long time, if it was ever alive. I remember flying to Bermuda on our honeymoon. We were talking, about what I don't know, but I glazed over while he was in mid-sentence. I realized in that instant, I'd made the dumbest decision in my life. We had nothing in common. He never read a book. Never enjoyed a good meal, or culture, or caring. He was the meanest, most insecure, most self-centered man I'd ever encountered. We shared not one interest until our children came along.

I know it's a terrible thing to admit, but at this moment, I wonder, *Why didn't I get off that airplane running and screaming? Why did I choose so poorly?* Mother found herself a wonderful man in Daddy. Is it because of what Honor says? Did I intentionally search out the one man who'd have nothing to do with God? I suppose I got what I asked for, then, didn't I? Oh, this is all too much right now.

I turn to look out the window. Wayne still has no idea that I know what he did to Honor.

What he did to Honor.

No wonder she left me. No wonder she wanted to get out of town—as far as she could from him. What kind of man makes a pass at his wife's sister, for crying out loud? What kind of man did I marry? What kind of man did I choose as the father of my children?

The same kind of man that beats you, says the voice in my head. *He's not a real man.* It's Honor's voice. I can hear her still. She is alive and well.

31

Alice

Dying persons often need closure or permission to die from loved ones. Assure them that all is forgiven, that their life had meaning, and that they will not be forgotten.

It's time. It's happening. Orange light is streaming in through the window, suspending specks of dust in the air. It's December 16, 5:32 p.m. Honor is dying. Right now.

I have been by her side for an eternity. I have been here for five days and four nights while Christmas carols played on car radios and presents got wrapped in warm, toasty homes.

Melody is here, and so is Sarah. The nurses and doctors have left us alone. Honor is in the same position she's been in for days. She is emaciated. Her eyes are closed. Her face is sucked in, her mouth twisted to the side. She doesn't look like herself anymore. I don't see the little girl so full of spit and energy. I don't see the young lady who searched for meaning and fought off men. I no longer see the woman, the gentle, loving, sensitive woman who carried her burden silently and cared for me like no other. She's not here anymore. My sister is somewhere between here and there. She's waiting.

I wonder if there are angels in the room with us. I wonder if Honor can hear singing that I can't hear. Are they calling her home? I cannot believe this is happening.

I know she is dying. I think I understand that as much as I am able. She is dying because we stopped feeding her days ago. I suffered over that decision. They told me it was the only humane thing to do. That her body is eating itself alive. Now she is starving to death.

Honor is peaceful. It is quiet here except for sweet sobs. Sarah is at my right side near the window. She's sitting in the chair leaning over to Honor, holding her hand. Melody is to my left. She is on her knees on the hard floor, her face buried in the pale blue blanket.

I am holding Honor's feet. I want to give her some space, some room to breathe. She's wearing white tennis socks. I brought a whole pack of clean ones from home, and I've been putting on a new pair each day. Her feet have not changed. They are still beautiful, graceful lines with high arches.

I am rubbing her legs. They're cool to the touch. I feel the smoothness of them. I shaved them for her last night, a ritual. I brushed her hair, washed her face. I have been preparing her. Preparing myself. Honor never woke up, but I think she knows. She knows I'm here. She knows it's time.

"It's okay," I tell her, finding my voice. "Honor, it's okay. We're all here. Sarah and Melody, and me, Alice. Honey, we're all here. It's all right."

Honor stays silent. As if she would say anything.

I hear a knock at the door.

"Miss Alice? Lord, I hope you don't mind. I know you're in the middle but—well, she asked me to sing for her," says Nurse Sadie, moving slowly to me. "Your sister? Honor asked me to sing—when it was time."

I'm not sure how I feel about this. About her. This should feel like an intrusion on our privacy, on our family, on the most severe moment we've ever endured, yet it doesn't feel that way. I welcome her with my eyes. This feels right, her being here.

Sadie finds a spot behind me, and begins humming soulfully. It's the sound of mourning. It's the sound of jubilation, a spiritual sound that fills the room as if church is now in session.

When I've done best I can, I want a crown . . .

"You can go on to heaven, Honor," I say, finding my calm. "You can go home. We love you, Honor. We love you so much."

I cannot believe my eyes. A single tear is rolling slowly down Honor's cheek. For days I've begged for a sign from her. And now I have it. She knows. *Oh, thank you!* She hears me. "It's okay," I tell her.

When I've done best I can, I want a crown

When I've done best I can, Lord, my crown . . .

She hears the voice of an angel, and I hear it too. It's time.

"We love you, Aunt Honor," says one of the girls, I'm not sure which.

"We love you. We love you, Honor. *I* love you," I tell her urgently. "Goodbye, my baby. My sweet baby girl. I will see you so soon, Honor Marie. I promise. I love you forever, Honor. I love you. *I love you.* Forever and ever."

Amen.

I am destroyed. The girls are beside themselves, but it is very quiet here except for the humming. It echoes in my soul. We have fallen off the face of the earth in this room, all of us, the grievers, in this cell. I am telling Honor it's okay to die now.

And then she is gone, warm sand through my fingers.

Now she is *gone.*

And I am still here.

I have not moved. Honor's body is gone, they took it away. My children have gone home, I think. I'm not sure. I have not moved. I am stone. I've become a fixture, melted into the walls with so many other loved ones who've said goodbye in this room. We are all here, embedded in the flowered wallpaper. We are not leaving. Cannot leave. Part of us will remain in this room forever.

The door swings open. Out of the corner of my eye, I see someone walk in. It's a woman. She bends down and places her black hand on my knee, red fingernails, rhinestone studs. This is Nurse Sadie.

"You gonna be all right, baby," she tells me as if she's sure of it. "Your baby sister loves you still. You got to know, death ain't a ditch you can jump over, but it don't mean it's all over. No sir. Honor's life has just begun. She's just started livin'."

I don't look up, but my eyes flood and go blurry.

"She left you one more letter, Miss Alice. She ain't done speakin' to you. Her words live on."

She places a folded piece of paper carefully in my hands and I open it immediately.

I look up at her. "Did you write this?" I ask.

"I wrote it for her when she couldn't write no more. You go on and read it while I tidy up now. Don't mind me."

I put my eyes on the paper and try to focus. Sadie begins humming quietly as she pulls the linens off the bed and shuffles around the room.

"Wade in the water. Wade in the water," she sings. "Wade in the water, God's gonna trouble the water."

I focus and read:

Listen, Alice. When I've gone on to heaven—

"If you should get there before I do, God's gonna trouble the water . . ."

—*make a pot of strong black coffee at midnight. Don't water it down. I'll come back to you in that darkest hour, I promise.*

"Tell all my friends that I'm a-comin' too. God's gonna trouble the water."

I'll stay till morning comes. We can go out in the yard and dance in the moonlight like when we were girls. Secret things shine true in the glare of the moon.

"Wade in the water. Wade in the water, children, God's gonna trouble the water."

Embrace the darkness, Alice. There's freedom in it.

I will see you on the other side. I promise. But I'm tired. I'll wait for you. They are going to call you now.

Your loving sister forever,

Honor

32

*Murrells Inlet
December 19, 2006*

Alice

I have cancelled Christmas. There is nothing I want to celebrate. I want the smell of cinnamon to air out of my home. I want the tree down, the lights put away, the presents taken back. I don't want to eat. Don't want the casseroles and breads and coffee cakes that neighbors have dropped by the house. I want none of it.

I just want Honor back.

I have put the obituary in the newspaper. I have met with the funeral home. I have picked out Honor's coffin and chosen an outfit for her to wear—a navy pant suit with pearl earrings and Great-Grandmother Miriam's cameo.

I have dressed her in these clothes, seen her naked body, felt her stiff hands. I have watched them apply makeup to her face. Her hair looks like an old lady's. She would hate it, but there's nothing I can do.

Now, I am sitting here, waiting for the funeral to be over with. I am sick to death of crying, of dying.

I am of no use to my daughters. They are sustaining me, feeding me, helping me put one foot in front of the other. Wayne has said very little. He has stayed out of my way.

We have no church, but I asked the little chaplain who looks like Radar on *M.A.S.H.* to perform the service. He seems like a good choice. Respectable.

I am untouchable to myself.

Look at Honor, lying there in that coffin. That is not her. There is one thing I know for sure: Honor is not there anymore. She is not in that body. Never again. I dressed her because I needed to know that Honor was truly gone. She is nowhere around here. I wonder, *If I lay down at her headstone, can I become the living dead?* Can I bring her back? She is a little girl for me again, in my head. The only thing that is real is a distant memory—us, as little girls.

After the service, we put Honor's coffin in the ground. There is a large oak tree nearby, providing shade. She would like this. She would like the breezes coming off the water. She would like the smell of pluff mud and the egrets flying over-head. This is the most peaceful I've ever seen her. But I am a sea of unrest.

On the ride home, I fully expect Honor to speak with me as if she's sitting in the back seat beside Sarah and Melody. *Nice service*, she might say. Or, *Why'd you have to dress me in navy? I'm a summer, Alice. Not a winter.* If Honor is truly gone, then where is she? Where did she go? Surely her spirit would stay with me. I allowed myself to believe this fairytale. After laying Honor to rest, I am devastated all over again as the tires slosh though puddles but no voice speaks to me from the great beyond.

January 2, 2007

I sent my girls back to school today. Wayne and I drove them to the airport. They left tearfully. They told me to take care of myself. I hated seeing them suffer like that. I wished I could do something to ease their pain, to make myself look better, feel better, become a fraction of my previous self again, for them. But I couldn't. I can't. I am on some strange ride where someone other than me is doing the driving, and I simply can-not get off.

I look at my husband of twenty-two years. Twenty-two years of my life sit there in that beer belly. "Alice, get me a beer, would ya?" he says.

I'm unable to move.

Then, "Alice! Get me a dad-gum beer! I'm thirsty in here!"

He tried to seduce my dead sister. He had affairs with women. Many of them. I think I always knew. Didn't I?

I am pondering the years when he would stay out late at work. Was he sleeping with those women then? While I was getting the kids in bed? I am in the middle of wondering these things when something wrenches my arm and pain shoots through my left shoulder.

Wayne yanks me out of my chair and grabs me by both arms, squeezing the fat that is loose above my elbows.

"Dangit, Alice! Snap out of it! She's been gone for a week now. She's gone!"

I am leaving my body. I am a couple of inches above the ground, dangling in his bear clutch. He shakes me. *Just put me down. Put me down.*

"Let go," I say through my teeth. Wayne seizes up as if I've woken him from a dream, a Jekyll and Hyde stupor. He sets me down, but doesn't let me go. Now he's crying.

"Alice, oh, honey! I'm so sorry, Alice. This has been hard on me too. I just . . . I need you, Alice. I need my girl ba-a-a-ack!" He hugs me close and falls to his knees, blubbering in my stomach. I am glad he put me down. Glad he didn't hit me this time.

I feel stinging on the back of my arms still, but other than that, I feel absolutely nothing.

Wayne is asleep. He drank too much and is snoring loudly in the next room. I've read Honor's papers again from start to finish. I feel like there are clues in there. Like hieroglyphics concealing my fate. I sit at the kitchen table and set the last letter down on the others, then force them into a neat pile, rhythmically tapping on all the sides until each one is perfectly straight. Then I wrap my sweater around my shoulders and stand up.

It's been nearly two weeks since Honor died. A new year has begun. A new year without Honor. I stare out the window into the blackness. My reflection is the only shape I can see. I see that I'm not crying. The tears are too far beneath the surface now. I can no longer reach them.

I remember my sister's words. *Make a pot of strong black coffee at midnight.* She wants me to wake up. *How could she know me so well?* She knew I would retreat into my shell when she died. She knew that my grief would burrow so deep inside me that I would begin to lose myself—that I might not recover from this blow. I don't care if I ever recover.

Embrace your darkest hour. Live through it. Feel everything there is to feel. I'll be there with you. I'll see you through till the morning comes.

My eyes burn. I stare at the clock. 11:51 p.m. It's almost midnight. I know what I need to do now. It's so very clear. There are suitcases to fill while Wayne is asleep, and what will I tell the girls? I walk to the counter and quietly fill a pot with water. Then I pour it in the coffee maker and flip the switch.

The heavenly rich aroma surrounds me and pricks at my skin. I feel my blood pulsing through me. *I'm waking up, Honor. Have coffee with me.*

It's going be a long night.

33

Alice

The road to St. Anne's Isle is winding and dark, but there's a full moon above me. It's quiet in my SUV—it's fully healed now, much like my foot. It's quiet outside. I've only seen a handful of cars in the past couple hours. I hear the quiet *whoosh* of the trees as I go by.

I imagine Honor driving this road less than a year ago. I think of what must have been going through her mind. She was running from Brett. Wanted desperately to get away from him and the person she'd become with him. She was running from her past.

I am doing the same thing now, except I'm not running from my past any longer. I'm running toward something now. Not away from. Toward something. I have made a choice that will determine my future. I will live with this choice. I feel alive all of a sudden. I wonder, *Why have I slept through my nights instead of getting out in the dark like I'm doing now? Why do any of us sleep?*

The moonlight illuminates snaking waterways and marsh grass. I am getting closer. I come to a small bridge and see the "welcome to the island" sign with a seagull on it. I have the strange sense that I am coming home for the first time.

He is still sleeping back in Murrells Inlet. Wayne is still sleeping, but he'll know instantly when he wakes that I'm gone. Does he even know about St. Anne's Isle? I'm sure I never spoke to him about Honor's whereabouts. Although it might have slipped out at some point. And then again, he did track down Brett.

Let's just assume he will come for me. Come after me. I will find Officer Simmons first thing in the morning. That's the best I can do. And what about the girls? They're in school now. I will call them both and tell them the truth. They love their father, but they know how he is, who he is. I'm hoping they will be happy for me. Happy that I am choosing life. I make a mental note to ask the girls to notify college security. Just in case.

How many years have I lived this way? How could I choose this life? There must be more out there. Honor found it on St.

Anne's Isle. Her letters—she told me to come here. Didn't she? She wrote her spiritual lyrics for me. Now it is my time to escape.

Oh, Honor. *Where are you?* I hope to find you here. Find myself here. Again.

I've never been on this island, yet I feel like I know this place. The island is small. The houses around me, modest like Murrells Inlet. I wonder where Blondell lives. I wonder where the Duchess lives. Not far from here, I know this much.

I pull up to a large park by the water and stop the car. I sit in silence in the dark, listening to my shallow breathing. I look through the windshield and see a playground shimmering in the full moon. There is a blue cast over all the earth. The sun is thinking of rising again.

I open the car door and a symphony of frogs fills my ears. *She was here*, they sing. *Honor was here.*

I put my keys in my hand, one key through each knuckle, a homemade weapon like Daddy taught me. I feel the need to have a weapon. I wish I'd had a weapon all those years ago—

He's still asleep, Alice. Don't worry. Wayne doesn't know yet.

I stumble through sand, then the texture changes. I'm on dirt, mulch now. I find a park bench across from a circle of bamboo. I know this bench. This is where Honor tried to kill herself. I don't want to kill myself. Not at all. I feel a million miles removed from the woman I was in that hospital room. I feel an urgency to live now, more than at any other time in my life. Honor did this for me. She sacrificed herself for me.

Again.

I lean back and rest my head on the bench. I am the elder. I was supposed to protect my baby sister, but it was Honor who protected me. It is Honor who is still protecting me.

I look up into the night sky at the bright full moon. The stars form constellations—the Little Dipper and the Big Dipper, the Drinkin' Gourd. I remember Honor's ring shout. *You got to run,* she told me.

I have, Honor. I have.

I'm here.

I awake to the sounds of children calling, laughing. I feel the brisk January air flow up my nose, and I open my eyes and see a little girl with pigtails standing over me. She backs up a step when she sees I'm awake.

"Well, I'll be. Go on, Sabannah. Go play with yo' sistah." A large black woman is hovering over me too, hands on hips. I pull myself up.

"Willa?" I ask.

She studies me hard as if trying to place me. "No, I ain't Willa. Willa over there. You know Willa?"

"No, not exactly. I'm . . ." I can see she's one of the nannies Honor had written about, and my pulse races. I feel closer to Honor suddenly. This was the right thing to do. The right place to come. "I'm Honor's sister. Honor Maddox?"

The woman's face spreads into melted butter. "Honor? You Miss Honor's sistah?" She hops on one foot then the other. "Willa! Wil-la! Come quick. Honor's sister right here!"

I hear a collective squeal as the nannies look at me. Half of them run over. The other half are too old or in no shape to do anything but lumber.

"You're Honor's sister?" asks a tiny near-midget-sized woman in tight blue jeans. I know this has to be Ruby.

"I'm Ruby," she says, taking my hand in both of hers and shaking it vigorously. "How's Miss Honor doin'? She doin' all right?"

A large woman in a colorful shawl backhands Ruby on her arm and glares at her. The rest of the group looks solemn and understands that my coming here means Honor is definitely not doing all right.

"She—Honor passed away a couple weeks ago," I say. There, I said it. Look, I'm still here.

"Ah!" exhales one woman in a red and yellow scarf. She puts her hand up to her mouth and closes her eyes.

"Aw Laaawd! Lawd have mercy! Miss Honor!" Ruby begins to wail and then a couple others join in. My eyes fill up and think of running over.

"I'm Willa," says a kind, large face, breaking through the commotion and sitting next to me. She reminds me of Nurse Sadie with an extra hundred pounds and eyeglasses. She studies my face and I look down at her thick wrists, poking out from her sweatshirt. "You must be Alice," she says.

She knows me.

Thank you, Lord. It's good to be known.

They take me to Blondell's house first. We walk through the woods and down a dirt lane as if in funeral procession. Heads are hung low like the Spanish moss draped on oak trees around us. There's very little talking. Willa has my arm in hers. "Everybody loved your sweet sister," she says.

I recognize Blondell's house when I see it, as if I've been here in my dreams, although it's even smaller than I had pictured. The cold wind from the ocean has picked up, and the screen door is banging against its frame. The nannies wait on the lane as Ruby and Willa walk me past the statues of gnomes and saints, past the rusted mailbox and the lye that I'm sure is still buried beneath the soil. There is no evil in this place.

When Blondell opens the door, she looks as though she's been expecting me. Her hair is frost, pulled back tight behind her head, and her black glassy eyes can see right through me. Her lips spread into a large toothy smile, and she pulls me to her.

"Alice," she says, like a long-lost friend. "I sorry fa yo' loss. I gladdee fa see you." She pushes me back to arm's length and motions toward the dinette table. "Come sit down ya. I done mek us some coffee fa warm you."

I sit down in one of the metal chairs and notice a black tail flicking in the chair beside me. I peek under the table and see two round yellow eyes. Inky! I can't tell you what it means to see this cat. I wonder, *Is Honor's spirit in this cat?* It's a crazy thing to think, I know, but there it is. That's my honest thought. I reach my hand out to it, and the cat purrs while I rub the top of its head. It closes those eyes and rolls its head to the side, asking me to scratch its ears. I oblige eagerly, and I'm comforted for the first time since Honor's passing.

"Cat mus' like ya. Inky ain liked On'ry much."

"No?" I ask, surprised.

"No. Miss On'ry, she too ett up wit she-self to scratch nobody ear."

I'm shocked. Or am I? I think back on Honor's notes and it makes sense. Honor was consumed here. Consumed with herself. Although she did help the Duchess quite a bit . . .

I'm thinking hard while Blondell sets a cup in front of me. It's chipped. She turns the chipped part away, then pours steaming black coffee into the white porcelain. She sits down across the table from me and stares, her arms tucked in her lap like an eighteen-year-old debutante. Her face is thick leather framed in tiny white curls that meet at her widow's peak. Her neck is lined and chicken-like and moves when she talks. "Ya come fa visit or come fa stay?" she asks.

"I'm not sure," I tell her truthfully.

"Ya look like Miss On'ry, I tell ya. She love you like ya can't believe."

I smile and put my face down, afraid I'll cry and won't be able to stop.

"I'm so grateful. To you," I say. "You took her in, you saved her life. I can't tell you what it means. She thought so much of you."

"Mm hmm. Eb'ry chile need a mammy," she says, then stands and walks to the sink, gazing out the window. She breathes in deep and then lets it out. "Eb'ry mammy need a chile."

She cranes her long neck and turns to me, and her face is filled with the deepest affection. I watch as two tears roll into the crevices of her wide nose, and she puts her long, trembling hands out to me.

I go to Blondell and hug her hard then. She is frail and sturdy, all at once.

And the cat is curled around my ankle, and the smell of fresh coffee floats on by, and all of a sudden, I feel like I am home. I'm finally, gratefully, home.

34

Alice

I am quite the celebrity on the island. I've been paraded on front porches, under palmetto trees, to elders and young ones. The Gullah community has made me feel welcome. We wind along a road. I begin to see the changes Honor described—the houses becoming grander, taller, and shinier.

We are one row back from the ocean and I spot our pink destination. Blondell is walking slowly but purposefully, proudly beside me. She knows that the fact I am here means she did her job right. They all did. They left an indelible mark on my baby sister—enough to make me want to come here when I needed a place the most. They are proud to welcome me, I can tell.

Ruby is talking my ear off, telling me things my sister did. "And right over there's where Miss Honor painted this great big oak tree with this egret in it," she says. "Better than I could do, Lawd have mercy." Finally, we walk for a short spell when no one utters a sound. All I hear is the shuffling of feet and the crackling of twigs under toe. And I don't know why, but I feel the need to inject myself into this empty space.

"You know it's funny," I confide to Ruby, quietly, wrapping my arms around my waist. "Since Honor died I've had this feeling like she's with me—like an itch I can't get to. All that time, sitting with her in the hospital, I was telling myself that if she just passed over to the other side, I'd finally have my Honor back." A golf cart cruises by us carrying two beer-drinking men and their fishing poles. They wave at us and we wave back.

"I completely expected to hear Honor's voice as I was driving home from the funeral, as I was driving down to St. Anne's," I say. "Being with all of you, on this island, I thought for sure I'd find her here. Isn't that . . . silly?"

Ruby touches me on the wrist and stops, then moves in front of me while the others walk by. I look down at her, her eyes at chest level. "Miss Alice, what you sayin' ain't strange to me a'tall," she squeaks, very seriously. "'Round these parts, we see dead folk all the time. It's how you lookin' is all I can figger. Must be them haint blue eyes you got—good for keepin' the spirits away." She grabs my other hand and smiles just slightly like she knows something I don't, keeping her gaze on my face. "Seems to me, you got to close them eyes ever now and again and let the dead come back in. Let 'em know they welcome."

Haint blue eyes. I have haint blue eyes. It's one of those *a-ha* moments as if the heavens have opened up and revealed the root of my problems. It's all in how I look at things. My entire life, I've never allowed my ghosts to come back in. Here on St. Anne's, I welcome them. It's time we made peace once and for all.

I blink at Ruby and then put one foot in front of the other and round the corner to the Duchess' driveway. Not Ruby, nor Willa, nor Blondell accompanies me up the long set of stairs. Instead, I go on alone. My legs lift one by one as I steady myself, praying I won't find a naked woman when I knock on the door. I've never actually seen such a sight. But part of me is dying for her to be naked—exactly the way Honor described her to me. If she *is* naked then all the pieces of the puzzle will fall into place. This will all be a reality instead of just a dream. I am walking in my sister's footsteps. It is so much easier when someone else has paved the way.

I turn around and see many faces of native St. Anne's. They are every shade of black. Every one beautiful. They smile at me, wishing me well. They have warned me about the Duchess. They say she hasn't been doing well since Honor left. Say she didn't do well through the Christmas holidays. But she is still here, surviving in this island refuge.

Here goes.

I knock. How long should I wait? I knock again and peer in the window, but it's foggy and tarnished from the harsh salty air. I'm thinking of ringing the doorbell when I hear shuffling footsteps moving closer. They stop just feet from me, then the doorknob turns, and we meet at last.

"Anne?" I say when she opens the door. She's wearing pink linen pants, wrinkled like an elephant. Her black top is too tight around her waist, and to make it worse, she has a white stretchy belt leftover from the eighties amplifying her bulge. But at least she's clothed.

"Yes?" I can tell she's trying to figure out if she knows me or not, but before I tell her I'm Honor's sister she breaks into a squeal that could shatter glass. She grabs me and pulls me to her, hugging tight, then presses me away to study me, then pulls me back to her again. Finally, she is both joy and complete agony, and she says, "Are you . . . Alice? *The* Alice?"

I nod.

"Oh, Honor, sweetie. Has she—"

I nod again slowly, unsure of what the news will do to her. Her eyes turn sullen and she grabs the door and gives a sad wave to the crowd on her driveway, then she shuts it carefully behind her as if blocking out any other thought but me.

"Call me Duchess, honey," she says. "Everybody else does."

She takes my hand and pulls me to her living room. There are plates of leftover food sitting on the coffee table and clothes and towels strewn along the back of the sofa. I push them aside and we sit. The sliding glass door that leads to the back porch is open, and a winter breeze cleans out the air around us.

Duchess looks down at her knees and licks her fading lips as if weighing the words to follow. Then she stares at me with moist eyes and says slowly, "Your sister was a good girl. She was a true friend, you know. She and I, we were kindred spirits."

I start to say something to console her, but she shushes me.

"Alice, you *have* to know that we did everythin' we could to save your sister. She's the most stubborn human bein' to ever walk the face of this earth. And she did it her way. But if I could take it all back, if I could haul her kickin' and screamin' to the hospital, I would. I'd do anythin' to have our Honor back."

"I know that," I assure her. "I do know that. And I'm so sorry you had to go through all this."

"But you're here," she says, shaking my arm with urgency. "You're here—and not with him, I take it?"

"I'm here," I say. "Not with him."

The Duchess' eyes sparkle and she brushes her white curls away from them triumphantly. "Then every bit of this was worth it. Even sweet Honor could tell you that's the honest-to-good-ness truth."

My whole day—finding Blondell and the nannies, meeting Duchess and seeing this beautiful sea island—is like jumping into the pages of my favorite novel and having it all come to life around me.

Duchess asks me to make myself at home, and she goes into the kitchen to put on a pot of coffee. I can hear her clinking around in there, running water, then finally the popping and spitting of the machine. I walk into the library and sigh when I see the walls of books, just like Honor said. I run my fingers along them and move toward the light of the window. There's a soft, cozy chair nestled in between two bookshelves and across from it, where you'll only see it when you're seated, is a painting of a large bivalve shell, brilliant blues and turquoise. I reach out and touch it and observe the signature in the bottom right corner.

Honor, it reads.

Duchess finds me there and hands me a mug of hot coffee. She apologizes for the grinds floating loose on the top. Says it's still something she's getting the hang of, "these new-fangled coffee machines."

Seeing me eyeing Honor's painting, Duchess swells. "Come on, Alice," she says. "Have I got somethin' to show you."

We walk along hardwood floors and I stop when I see it, the buffet table in the hallway. I know this piece. There are three cozy chair scenes painted on top in ovals. One is a reading nook much like the library chair, the next shows two Adirondack chairs on the beach with umbrellas, and the last oval shows a rocking chair on the porch of a beach house. There's something so sad about this piece. The chairs are all empty.

"She was paintin' that for Mrs. Hutchinson right before she left," Duchess says. "It was all she could do to paint that thing. Never finished it, neither. See how the circles are just kinda floatin' there? Honor told me it wasn't done, so I wouldn't let Mrs. Hutchinson have it. I just kept it for myself. Not that Mrs. Hutchinson was real happy about that. You can have it if you want, Alice."

I touch the raised edges of the acrylic paint and tears sting my eyes. This is what Honor was painting while she was dying. I imagine every stroke of her brush. Duchess sees my anguish so she pulls me on.

"Come on, I got to show you somethin' else. The pièce de résistance!" I take a steaming sip and we walk through white columns to the gargantuan dining room. And in that moment, miracle of miracles, it happens.

I finally see Honor.

And not only see her, but I feel her, I hear her. She is real to me again.

Up on the wall is a very naked, yet attractive version of the Duchess stepping out of a shell. There are angels to the left and right of her, handing her clothing. But what takes my breath away are the two cherubs hovering over her head. One has Honor's face, her hands, her long flowing brown hair, and beside her, there is me. We are children again when all was innocent. We are angels.

Look at that, I hear Honor say finally, the sweet sound of an eight-year-old child in my ear. *Aren't they pretty, Alice?* she asks me. *That's you and me there. See, we're angels up there together. And we'll be on this wall forever, you and me. And we won't fall away. Don't worry 'bout that. I won't ever let it happen. Not ever.*

35

Alice

Not long after I came to St. Anne's Isle, I felt it necessary to call Waccamaw Memorial Hospital and tell Nurse Sadie thank you for all that she did for me, for Honor, while she lay dying.

It was one of those moments when the earth shifts as if you're standing on a fault line.

The hospital could not produce Nurse Sadie for me. In fact, they said no Sadie worked there, had worked there, nor had been involved in any way with Honor's care. I asked about hospice. Could she have been from hospice? They told me no. I asked about volunteers. Perhaps she was someone who came in under the radar. "No one comes in under the radar," they told me.

Nurse Sadie simply did not exist.

I spoke with my daughters about that day, the day Honor passed. They both remembered her voice, the song she sang, just like I do. And I've got Honor's letters where the handwriting changes. We've all been changed by this piece of news. If Nurse Sadie did not exist except for us, was she an angel? We choose to think so.

This choice to believe in something so impossible has been like finding a shiny white pearl while breaking open muddy oysters. It's something we cling to, this miracle of ours. It gives me faith, beyond a doubt, that my sister lives on. And it is this faith, and the very fact that I can speak of it now, that sustains me.

Officer Simmons has an unmovable faith in God, from what I can tell. And he is everything Honor had described. He is the warmest, most sincere man I've ever encountered. He lives several streets over from my small bungalow, and he helps me with manly things every now and again, repairing a roof leak or tilling the soil for my garden. He is a true friend, nothing more than that. I am not ready for anything more, nor will I be in the foreseeable future, yet his friendship has become quite important to me, I'll admit.

When Wayne finally figured out where I was, he came for me. But I wasn't there. Poor dear, the Duchess was home, yet I'm not sure who was more scared, Duchess or Wayne. She was naked as the day she was born. Wayne was arrested for banging down her door, and he spent the night in the local jail. I never saw him at all, but Michael did. That's Officer Simmons. I call him Michael.

"Quite a piece o' work you got there," Michael told me. "I doubt Mr. Man'll be coming back anytime soon."

Mr. Man. Ha. That made me laugh. I have no idea what was said or done to Wayne, but to my knowledge, he has not been back to the island in over a year. He has taken up with his secretary. She's living with him from what the girls tell me. Oh, they still see Wayne and talk to him. They need their father and he needs them, so I don't mind, not really. They are grown women now and can make their own decisions.

I am grown too. Living on my own is the most liberating experience. I spend my days working at the small bookstore on the island, and I love it. Books all day long, and interesting customers, new friends who love books as much as I do. When the girls came down for Christmas a few months ago, we had a real tree with ornaments just the way we wanted them, with Christmas carols and eggnog and no drunk husband to spoil the fun. It's the best holiday I could have asked for without Honor.

Duchess gave me that buffet table that Honor never finished, and it's sitting right here in my hall. I think of Honor every time I pass it and I tell myself I'll try to finish it for her one day. But I can't paint. I may never finish it. But that's okay. Seeing it with work to be done feeds my fantasy that Honor might paint on it again. In a way, I still have expectations that she'll walk through my door. I know it sounds crazy, but I'm just being honest. When someone you love so much dies, there is a part of you that embraces the magic of *what if*. There are parts of you that die right along with your loved one, but other parts that are awakened that you never knew existed. Like the belief in angels or a faith in the unknown. It's pure magic. That's the best way I can describe it.

Just after the divorce was finalized, I asked Blondell to take me to the spot in the woods where they held that ring shout for Honor the night before she left. I made sure to bring Duchess with me. I thought it might do her some good too. We walked slowly together under oak trees dripping with Spanish moss and came to a clearing near the marsh. I could see the Atlantic from where we stood, and I watched birds nibbling in the spartina grass, filling their bills. Blondell pointed with her walking cane to a circle in the grass that had worn thin as if a horse had been staked to the ground and walked around and around on a daily basis.

"Dis where we come," she confided in us. "Meet out ya mos' eb'ry week. Dis we praise house. Dis God house."

We were standing in God's house under the clear, open sky. There were no pews, no pulpit, no stained glass, no hymnals. And you know, I did look for the one man on earth who had nothing to do with religion. Honor was right. But I've learned here on St. Anne's that God is not religion. And God has nothing to do with men like Preacher Bullard, but everything to do with bowing oaks and soaring egrets and full moons that paint the world blue.

And magic. Pure magic.

As I stood in that clearing beside Miss Blondell and Duchess, in the middle of that etched circle in the ground, I could almost hear the echoes, feel the stomps of the feet that had moved around Honor. I could picture her, listening to the lyrics of the shout. Paying attention.

She heeded the call. She responded with the greatest escape.

To this day, my baby sister is the most courageous woman I've ever known. She remains with me on this island. I can feel her presence, like God's, in the marsh grass, in the water, in the pluff mud. And if I close my haint blue eyes for just a moment and truly believe, she says to me, *Oh Alice, look. We made it.*

Epilogue

June 4, 2008

Duchess

My good friend, Miss Blondell, told me the other day she thinks Alice is gonna be just fine. Not that anybody's ever "just fine" after they lose a loved one. I am certainly not fine after losing sweet Honor, but I know this much—she'd let me have it if she knew I was losing sleep over her. That's just the way she was though, tough like that. Tender like that too.

But Alice is strong like something I've never seen. I know what Honor was talking 'bout now. Alice has a well in her, a never-ending well that seems to fill up whenever she's running low. I dip into that well every now and again because just as I'm trying to look out for Alice, I can tell she's doing the same for me. Why, just this morning on her way to the bookstore, she dropped by here and brought me a sand dollar. Out of the blue.

"What's this for?" I teased. I knew full well why she'd brought it to me.

Alice just looked at me, not sure if I was mad, sad, or happy. "Oh. Don't you need to have shells every now and then to help you—"

"Mourn, you mean? Grieve, is that it?"

"Well, yes, I thought—"

I couldn't take that innocent scaredy-cat look on her face, so I lost it. I did! I burst out laughing. Slapped my thigh even.

"Why, Miss Alice, you are the sweetest thing I have ever seen. Thank you for my shell. I'm gonna put it right outside with the others."

She stood there waiting.

"You mean you want me to go right now?" I asked her.

"Only if you were planning on it," she said, "though I wouldn't mind going out there myself."

So the two of us climbed down my sun-beaten steps with the warm wind kissing at our cheeks. I led the way and knelt down at my "mound," what I call it. My mourning mound. And I set that pretty bleached-white sand dollar on top.

"You know we don't get very many like this—ones that are still whole," I told her.

"Yes, I know," Alice said, tucking her blonde hair behind her ear. "But I wanted to show you something. Watch this. This is special."

The waves crashed in front of us, letting off white froth that coated the earth, and before my very eyes, Alice took that round sand dollar in her two thin hands. She pressed down on each side and up in the middle. She strained with the pressure and then we both heard a *pop*. I knew what was 'bout to happen since I'd spent so much of my life on the beach, so I cupped my hands underneath hers as tiny white jagged shells fell down.

"Birds!" I squealed, delighted, and I looked at her. And Alice, God bless her, in that moment looked like her sister—the same sense of wonder, the glitter in her smile—and my eyes went moist.

"Thank you," I told her. "I truly needed that."

"So did I, Duchess," she said, wrapping her arm 'round my shoulder. "Sometimes broken things can be the most beautiful, you know. And there's a legend about the sand dollar."

"Yes, I know. That the doves inside are for spreading good will and peace," I said.

Alice looked over at me. "My mother used to tell me that same thing when I was little—when we were going to Sunday school. I haven't heard it in ages!"

I thought about telling her then. But I just couldn't. I couldn't do it.

Instead I looked back at the pile—at all the years that lay beneath it—and drew my hands out straight in front of me. Then I peppered my grief and guilt with those five doves of peace, scattering 'em from east to west.

Then the strangest thing happened.

Alice and I sat there in silence and watched as the spirit of Honor swirled up around us in a sandstorm. It was like the ocean rolled back her soul and all the others that had gone on to a better place. The spirits of my unborn children and of Mama sailed through the air with vigor, sending sand and dust, prickly like ice, to our faces.

The only soul I know for a fact wasn't there was my dearly departed husband's, Mr. Preacher Man, Mackey Bullard. No, his soul'll never see the light of day.

Yes, I know. I know I said I was married to the mayor of Muldoon, Idaho, but I've always been a liar. Always had to be to survive. We spent years getting chased from congregation to congregation. Mackey Bullard had quite the reputation, you know. And I'm so ashamed. Still to this day. He never admitted to it, but I knew deep down it was true—what he'd done to all those women, all those girls—and I never did a cotton-pickin' thing about it. I couldn't. What could I do? I was the preacher's wife. I'd been trained to keep my mouth shut.

Well, it's too late now. If anybody's ever suffered over guilt, it's me. My sin is the sin of silence. It likes to eat me alive when my guard is down. The only time I feel any better is when I'm naked to the world, to God, baring my ever-living soul.

Yes ma'am, I've had to make my peace with my past. With The Man Above. And my faith has never been stronger than it is this very day. I know for a fact God sent angels into my life to heal me, to protect me. How else could you explain it—those girls coming into my life again, one after the other?

And I'll never forget the day I figured out the truth about Honor—that the woman who'd come to *my* house for healing was the very same girl from Murrells Inlet who ended it all for me years ago. I remember feeling so grateful it was over back then. So glad Mackey was gone.

It wasn't hard to figure out. Soon as I saw her face, I suspected as much. She looked so much the same, just her hair was shorter and she was a woman now. But Honor's green eyes were something I'd never forget.

Glory, I hated leaving Murrells Inlet. I loved it there with the water and sea breezes and Southern hospitality. I loved Honor's mama and daddy too. They were real friends. Mackey and I never made real friends—we weren't anywhere long enough to make them.

And I loved those two girls of theirs, though they didn't give a hoot about me. You know, I never could have children myself. I wasn't lying about that. My babies died before they were born. That's my sentence, I suppose. But Alice and Honor, they grew on me. I loved them like my very own. And then I had to leave. Plumb broke my heart.

I knew what had happened. I knew what Mackey'd done. I'd heard the accusations so many times before. And I always suspected it wasn't an accident that killed him neither. I'd just hoped for Honor's sake it wasn't true.

I didn't know the truth about Mackey's death for all those years until Honor revealed her deepest, darkest secret to me. I remember the shadows dancing like spirits all over the walls from the candlelight flickering in Blondell's bedroom. I thought I'd get ill when I realized how much Honor'd suffered, and I wanted to tell her who I was then. Tell her how sorry I was. Honest I did. But I couldn't. I was just as guilty as he was for never stopping it.

But I had to do something so she wouldn't find out about me, so she wouldn't stop caring for me. I made sure every picture of Mackey disappeared and locked them up tight in that little room in the garage where Fluffy is, God rest her soul. I stuck them right behind Fluffy.

I just pray Alice never figures it out. There are some secrets I got to keep just a little while longer. Honor is gone, but she made peace in this life before she left. I'd like to think I had something to do with that. I think with a little time, Alice can do the same, can start a new life here on St. Anne's, not chained down by memories of what Mackey did to her, what her husband did to her.

Miss Blondell knows all about me though. Has known for years. I had to tell somebody lest I pop, but she'll never tell. She swore it. And she's a woman of honor—a woman of her word and the wisest woman I know.

I know there's no excuse for the bad that happens, the things that go wrong in this world, but I do know one thing for a fact: God can use every bit of it. If I ever doubted—which I did many times—I don't now. The Lord brought my babies back, Honor and Alice. And I'm no saint, but He's given me a second chance. I'll never let anything hurt 'em again.

When that sandstorm rose up around me and Alice, we didn't hunker down and hide. No. We sat up straight with arms out wide, holding hands, and embraced our loved ones, the ghosts of our past. It was like tipping our heads into heaven for a second. Then before we knew it the sand had settled down and it all washed out to sea again with the tide. But we knew they'd been here with us. They're here in this place right now, on St. Anne's. They touched our lives. And we'll never forget. Not ever. As long as we live.

A Note from the Author

I am blessed to live in the South Carolina Lowcountry. The people, culture, and beauty of this place inspired this book. I hope you get the chance to visit Murrells Inlet, the "Seafood Capital of South Carolina." If you love fresh seafood, you'll be in heaven with over thirty restaurants in a four-mile strip! But if you're looking for a secluded getaway, St. Anne's Isle, I'm sad to say, is a fictitious location—though I'd love to go there myself. It is, however, based on the many Sea Islands that dot the South Carolina coastline, home to remaining Gullah/Geechee populations. Miss Blondell, Ruby, Willa, and the nannies are just a taste—

visit the Lowcountry to experience the fascinating Gullah/Geechee culture yourself. For information and resources, visit my Web site, www.nicoleseitz.com, or visit the Gullah/Geechee Sea Island Coalition at www.officialgullahgeechee.info for information on authentic efforts to keep the Gullah/Geechee culture alive and the people on their homeland.

This book, in its entirety—including the characters and events—is a work of fiction, although sections of chapter 10 have been adapted from actual unpublished writings of my aunt Bonnie's that I found while doing research. In many ways, writing this novel was a healing process for me. Aunt Bonnie, who died in 1996 of cancer, didn't tell family members about her illness until shortly before her death. Although this book is fiction, I wanted to examine reasons why a person might choose to keep such a devastating secret.

In *Trouble the Water*, Honor Maddox develops a form of cancer called Inflammatory Breast Cancer (IBC). I had never heard of this cancer before doing my research, and in fact, most people have never heard of it. However, IBC is the most lethal form of advanced breast cancer, comprising up to 5 percent of all breast cancer cases. The problem with IBC is that it goes against everything we've learned. Typically "lumps" are not present as the cancer presents in "sheets." Many times, the disease is mistaken for mastitis, a breast infection, and antibiotics are prescribed. Other times it's dismissed as an allergy or bug bites. Often, by the time a correct diagnosis is made, the cancer has metastasized, spreading to other organs.

Below are some typical symptoms of IBC as listed by the Inflammatory Breast Cancer Research Foundation:

- Rapid, unusual increase in breast size
- Redness, rash, blotchiness on breast
- Persistent itching of breast or nipple
- Lump or thickening of breast tissue
- Stabbing pain and/or soreness of breast
- Feverish breast
- Swelling of lymph nodes under the arm or above the collarbone
- Dimpling or ridging of the breast
- Flattening or retracting of nipple

If you experience any of these symptoms, ask your doctor about an MRI or biopsy as IBC may not be detected by mammogram or ultrasound. And please remember: *You don't have to have a lump to have breast cancer.*

For more information on Inflammatory Breast Cancer (IBC), visit my Web site for a comprehensive list of resources, www.nicoleseitz.com, or visit the IBC Research Foundation at www.ibcresearch.org.

Peace and blessings,

Nicole

Reading Group Guide

1. Duchess says one thing she knows for sure is this: "A woman can't be an island, not really." Discuss the concept of woman as an island. Do you agree with what she said?

2. The Gullah/Geechee community of St. Anne's Isle opens its arms to Duchess, Honor, and her sister, Alice. What might have happened if Blondell and the nannies had not embraced these women, leaving them to their own devices?

3. Why does Blondell send Honor to go stay with the Duchess?

4. Honor and Duchess did not raise children of their own, yet longed for them. How does this affect them as women? What about Blondell?

5. What is Honor's relationship with authority figures? Who are these figures in her life? How do these relationships affect the way she views herself and relates to others? Who are the authority figures in your own life?

6. Honor, Duchess, and Alice each have secrets in this book. What are they? Why do they keep these secrets? What are the effects of secrets in our lives?

7. Duchess says, "[*Trouble the Water*] is the story of Honor, come and gone, and how one flawed woman worked miracles in this mixed-up world." Is it possible for good to come from another's mistakes? Can you think of any real-life examples?

8. When we first meet Alice, she describes her "tidy shoebox of a life." By the end of the book, does her life transform into something else? If so, why?

9. In *Trouble the Water*, seashells and water have strong spiritual symbolism. Can you identify any other symbolic themes in the book?

10. Alice does not find out about Honor's physical issues until very late. How does Alice feel about not being told? How would you feel? Are Honor's reasons for not telling Alice valid? Have you ever known someone who kept an illness secret? What were the consequences?

11. Sisterhood is a strong theme in this book. Examine Alice's and Honor's relationship as sisters. Now examine other "sister" relationships in the novel.

12. Do you believe Alice knew the truth about her husband, Wayne, all along? If so, why does she stay in the relationship?

13. Who do you think Sadie was? What does Alice believe? Why is this important to her future?

14. There is a theme of endings as new beginnings in this book. Please discuss.

15. What does it mean to "trouble the water"? Discuss Honor's, Alice's, and Duchess' "diseases" and healing in this book. What are their "symptoms"?

5/08